Vengeance Rides the River

The murder of Dave Lockhart's wife by a set of desperados who plague the Red River country of Texas leads him to a desperate mission for revenge.

Though he was once a soldier, Lockhart is no natural killer, but his quest for revenge becomes marked by murder, bullets and gun-smoke, and brings him face to face with deadly men.

Then he meets Helen, who must overcome difficulties that few women ever face. Now she must teach Lockhart that there can be a world of difference between vengeance and justice. . . .

Vengeance Rides the River

HUGH MARTIN

A Black Horse Western

ROBERT HALE · LONDON

© Hugh Martin 2010
First published in Great Britain 2010

ISBN 978-0-7090-8959-9

Robert Hale Limited
Clerkenwell House
Clerkenwell Green
London EC1R 0HT

www.halebooks.com

Typeset by
Derek Doyle & Associates, Shaw Heath
Printed and bound in Great Britain by
CPI Antony Rowe, Chippenham and Eastbourne

CHAPTER ONE

RAIDERS' RAMPAGE

Ice-cold alarm skewered into Dave Lockhart's guts the moment he saw the sign of mounted activity in the dust of the side trail leading to his homestead.

He pulled rein to halt his horse and slanted himself in the saddle to take a closer look at the ground. His years of desert campaigning with the cavalry had equipped him with the ability to translate the prints of mounted traffic and the import of what he saw was plain as day. Several horses had passed on the way to the homestead, then there was an overprinting that indicated returning animals.

He spotted an ominous brownish-red blotch, almost wholly dried but unmistakably blood. Someone among the riders, unless it was one of the horses, had been bleeding profusely enough to leave such a trace on the trail.

The passage of several horses in this obscure and rarely visited spot could only mean that Dal Colquitt's gang of ruthless marauders had visited.

Lockhart had just left the town of Blue Brush where he found a panicky rumour rippling through the populace. Colquitt's brutal and elusive bunch had swooped and robbed another bank somewhere at this end of Texas. No one knew exactly where. It was just a rumour, seemingly gleaned from someone passing through, but it quickly spawned another rumour that the gang might be headed this way, perhaps scooting for Indian Territory across the Red River.

It was popularly believed that the ghostlike Colquitt bunch had their mysterious hideout somewhere among the Indian Nations, but the forces of law and order had not yet discovered it. Nor had they yet come to grips with the gang who appeared abruptly and struck hard and bloodily before disappearing as speedily as they had arrived.

What Lockhart saw, virtually on his own doorstep, bore out the tale about their running for the Red River after their raid on the bank. He saw no trace of a party of riders on the main trail from town, so they must have come up the trail from the south, which would be consistent with the Red River and the Indian Nations being their goal. They had taken time out to detour to his homestead, possibly in search of grub or water or simply plunder. The smoke from the chimney had probably given away the isolated position of the homestead.

And Lockhart had left his wife, Marcy, alone at the house!

Cursing his decision that morning to go to the hardware store in town in search of a bolt to replace a broken one on the shaft of his buckboard, he frantically spurred his mount towards his home.

He reached the yard fronting the frame house, had only a blurred and confused impression of the door standing wide open before the breath gusted out of him as his whole attention was taken by the horrifying sight of Marcy lying face down at the bottom of the porch steps. Her arms were stretched out and she gripped the Winchester they kept loaded in the house in case of some emergency. A crimson pool had spread out from under her.

He hurled himself from his saddle, pounded across the yard and squatted beside her. Emotion almost choked him but some calm portion of his consciousness made him almost see what had occurred. The bank raiders must have appeared here and Marcy, always feisty and brimful of courage, must have taken the Winchester from its rack over the fireplace and attempted to defend the place from the porch.

Lockhart took hold of her head tenderly, brushed away the curtain of silky, light-brown hair that had fallen across her face Her eyes were closed and she looked like a sleeping child. Then he realized that she was still alive and breathing shallowly and he clutched her closer to him, forcing back his sobs.

Her eyes fluttered open, stared up at him, blankly at first, then recognition dawned in her face.

'Marcy, what happened? Who did it?' Lockhart asked in a quivering voice. 'Was it Dal Colquitt's gang?'

His wife nodded. Her lips moved soundlessly then she managed to gasp a few painful, struggling words. He pressed her closer to him, striving to hear.

'Dave . . . the boy . . . the fair-haired boy. . . .' The words faded but she raised her hand with difficulty and indicated her right temple. 'The boy . . . hit here . . . I shot . . . wounded . . . that boy . . . the one with the calico horse,' she gasped. Then her gasping voice faltered again. She tried to grasp Lockhart's shirt but and her hand fell away limply. Her eyes closed again, and she gave a soft, almost whispering, sigh.

Lockhart knew she was dead and, feeling detached from the whole world for some unknowable length of time, he squatted there with her head held close against his chest, unheeding of her blood seeping into his clothing.

When he could think at all, he tried to fathom her gasping, broken message. It was something about a fair-haired boy and a calico horse among the bunch of raiders. So far as he could piece her disjointed sentences together, she shot the youngster, wounding him in the temple.

8

He must have been the one who shot her down. Marcy was trying desperately to identify to him the man who had perpetrated her murder. She had plainly wounded him in the right temple, a fact that Lockhart grasped and held on to as an essential clue.

Somewhere among the Colquitt bunch there was a youngster, probably some gun-happy young thug who, if he had not subsequently died from the wound, was probably marked by it. It seemed plain enough: a fair-haired kid on a calico mount, running with Dal Colquitt's bunch and with a wound that would clearly identify him. Even when healed, it would probably leave a betraying scar. A man so marked could be found.

Still holding his dead wife's head close against his chest and with tears blurring his vision, Dave Lockhart vowed aloud in a rasping, emotional croak: 'I'll find him, Marcy. I'll find him and kill him – even if I have to kill the rest of Colquitt's gang as well!'

He began to move like a man in a trance, afterwards hardly being able to recall how he lifted Marcy, carried her into the house and laid her on the bed.

As he entered, he vaguely noticed the vindictive splintering of wood on the frontage of the house, indicative of the raiders having fired on the premises, probably on their arrival, to intimidate the household.

He made a tour of the place, noting in a half-aware fashion that they had raided the kitchen, taking food. In the bedroom closet, he found his Colt .45, holstered in its full shell-belt and his only box of ammunition. The marauders had not discovered it nor had they taken the Winchester that Marcy had carried, which suggested they had wanted rations for the trail and had not been raiding for arms.

With his lean face drawn into a hard mask of determination, he belted the weapon around his waist. He had scarcely worn it since he quit his post-army cattle-trail wanderings and, having found Marcy, settled for a homesteader's life. His ultimate hope was that he might develop this little place into a modest horse ranch, but now, his horizons had changed.

He went outside again to inspect the corral at the rear of the house, expecting to find that the raiders had stolen his two draught horses kept there but the animals were still there. Food seemed to have been the whole object of the attack, but the raiders never reckoned on a woman of Marcy's fighting spirit being on the place, ready to defend it.

Lockhart was haunted by the notion that someone among the Colquitt bunch, quite possibly the fair-haired kid whom his wife had managed to wound in the temple, had made some attempt to molest her.

'That damned fair-haired kid – I'll track him to the ends of the earth and kill him!' he growled aloud as he set about releasing the draught pair from the corral and hitching them to the buckboard wagon.

With deliberate movements but still acting like a man in a trance, he returned to the house and brought out Marcy's body wrapped in a blanket, managing also to include a pillow in his burden. He laid her tenderly in the wagon with her head on the pillow, smoothed back her tangled fair hair, tucked the blanket around her as if settling a sleeping child in its bed. For a full minute he looked at her. Her face was calm and, in spite of the blood already seeping through the blanket, she appeared to be only sleeping and was as beautiful as on the joyful day he first met her in the flowering of her youth.

Lockhart climbed up to the seat and set the pair of horses in motion. The shaft with its faulty bolt creaked as the wagon rumbled over the hoof-mauled surface of the yard. He had neither the inclination nor the time to replace the bolt with the one he had purchased in town, still in the pannier of his saddle horse. He hoped the bolt would hold in position until he reached Blue Brush. Crouched broodingly over the reins, he cursed the bolt and the creaking shaft. Had it not been for them, he would not have gone into town, leaving Marcy alone.

Then he cursed himself for his spur-of-the-moment decision to repair the fault. The whole thing could have waited and he would have been present to defend the homestead.

A crushing weight of blame for Marcy's fate

descended on him.

Savage self-reproach took hold of his whole being. Why, he asked himself, had he been fool enough to leave her alone on the place? He knew damned well that this was as brutal a time as any in the turbulent history of Texas.

The Civil War had slashed scars across the whole state. The victorious Union had punished the former unswervingly rebel Texas by putting it under severe military occupation, which had only recently ended, leaving a boiling legacy of resentful lawlessness.

Additionally, there was in some sections of the population a general brutality engendered by the decades-long war against the Comanche Indians who bore a long and bitter resentment of intrusion by settlers.

Then came the outlaws, rampaging around not only Texas but the neighbouring partially settled regions of Indian Territory and Oklahoma Territory as well: bitter, disaffected men with bloody histories and savage habits acquired in the war. Texas might hope to settle itself into an ordered, perhaps ultimately prosperous post-war life as cattle-ranching and farming struggled to flourish but the gun-heavy riders of the owlhoot trails were ever haunting the margins.

They were a menace, ever ready to charge in on honest endeavour, greedy for plunder and backing their greed with bullets. The Lone Star State's characteristic enforcers of the law, the Texas

12

Rangers, fought the tide of lawlessness with only limited success.

The land was rife with danger in this struggling age. Dave Lockhart needed no reminding of that fact, yet he had foolishly and unthinkingly let his guard down briefly.

Now, he carried the corpse of his young wife as the result of his stupidity.

People on the straggling street of Blue Brush saw the buckboard come slowly into town and their attention was at once taken by Lockhart's demeanour. He was lean, in his late thirties and still had some of the dash and style of a horse-soldier about him.

Under the broad brim of his black sombrero, his face, burned and seamed by harsh weathers, was drawn into an expression speaking eloquently of both anger and grief.

There were many in town who knew that Dave Lockhart, a peaceful homesteader, had once been a cavalryman and had also worked as a cow-wrangler, taking beef up the trails to the brawling Kansas railheads but in their experience, these days he never carried a gun. Now, he was sporting a Colt .45 and was plainly disturbed and belligerent with blood soaking the front of his shirt.

When the citizens on the street caught sight of the blanket-covered form lying on the wagon bed, they gathered around the vehicle.

Lockhart reined the team. 'My wife!' he announced in a throaty croak. 'Dal Colquitt's gang swooped on my place while I was here in town and killed my wife!'

The news spread through the town as if by electric telegraph and the knot of townsfolk around the buckboard became a small crowd to which the mayor of Blue Brush, Harry Treeton, and town marshal Lew Cox, were attracted.

A hush descended on the gathering and into it Lockhart spilled out his story in a hoarse and quivering voice.

'That tale about Colquitt's bunch robbing a bank somewhere at this end of the state was true and they stopped off at my place, killed Marcy and stole grub,' he gulped.

He gave the crowd an emotion-torn account of Marcy lying in the yard with the rifle in her hands, having obviously tried to hold the raiders off and of his sense of the violation of everything he valued.

'We must get them. This could happen again to any of us – to any of your wives!' he declared 'They must have headed for the Red River; they'd hardly go south, deeper into Texas, with the alarm raised. They might still be somewhere near enough to be caught up with before they cross into Indian Territory. Before she died, my wife identified the one who shot her. He's a fair-haired youngster. Marcy injured him with a shot. He'll be marked by a wound to the head and he's on a calico horse – and I want to find him.'

'Now, hold hard, Mr Lockhart," interjected Mayor Treeton. 'What are you suggesting?' He

14

sounded hesitant.

'Why, raising a citizens' posse and going after them and settling things with Colquitt's bunch – and particularly with that fair-haired kid. Damn it, you must understand how I want to get that kid!' stated Lockhart angrily. 'We've got a marshal and his deputies and there are enough men in this town to form a strong posse.'

'A posse would be useless by this time,' said Mayor Treeton, attempting to soothe him. 'Most likely they'll be far away, probably well across the Red River and deep in the Indian Nations, if that's where they really do have their hideout.'

'And you know my jurisdiction ends with the town limits,' put in Marshal Cox, sounding as hesitant as the mayor. The whole town seemed to have cold feet.

'You mean you're not willing to try!' accused Lockhart hoarsely.

'Look,' said Cox defensively, 'catching up with the Colquitts out yonder is properly a matter for the Texas Rangers and the US marshals and, over in Indian Territory, for Judge Parker's federal marshals and the US Indian Police. We're shocked by what's happened to your wife. The whole town feels outraged and you can count on our full support—'

'You talk about your full support but nobody's willing to come out and help track down this murdering bunch!' finished Lockhart, scowling and almost snarling at the gathering. 'You talk about the

US marshals and the Texas Rangers but Colquitt's bunch has been rampaging around this end of the state for months. Yet the law has not caught up with them. Now it's come to this and this whole town has no intention of doing anything about it!'

'Now, see reason, Lockhart,' said Cox. 'Mayor Treeton is right. They're probably out of Texas by now and far beyond catching by any posse of amateurs. I figure you brought your wife into town so she can be accommodated in the funeral parlour and you can arrange her funeral. Why not attend to that business first? I'll telegraph the Rangers' headquarters and put out word about what happened at your place. Why, after the bank robbery, the Rangers are probably already investigating the case.'

'And getting nowhere, as usual,' snorted Lockhart.

He tried to gulp back his choking anger, glowered at faces that were sympathetic yet manifestly stolidly resistant. Plainly not one of these men, his nearest neighbours, was willing to help him. Then his rage came out in full, uncontrolled spate.

'Damn the lot of you!' he snarled. 'Are you all cowards? I know there are men here who were not afraid to spend years at war, so where's your fighting spirit now? For years I've been listening to Texans boasting of their readiness to defend their kith and kin and homes and I've heard such talk in this very town. Now there's murder on your doorstep and the proud town of Blue Brush shows itself to be yellow!'

At a later date Dave Lockhart could acknowledge that, charged by emotion, he was probably unreasonable in his expectations of immediate action from the citizens, for he had made his challenge a bit late in the day, when the Colquitts must surely have been far away.

Blue Brush folk were not without fighting spirit but they had small-town logic. To them, there was no point in chasing an enemy who, quite obviously, could not be caught. At that moment, though, in front of a gathering of those he vainly hoped would rally to a call for action, Dave Lockhart wished he had settled anywhere but Blue Brush.

Still fuming, he forced himself to accept Marshal Cox's advice about attending to his immediate needs concerning his wife's death, since he had no other choice.

For the next three days, he disciplined himself to clamp down his anger and anxiety and went about arranging her funeral with the town's undertaker.

After Marcy's body was taken into the funeral parlour, Lockhart had the marshal telegraph a message to her only surviving relative, her brother, Jack, a lawyer in St Louis, who eventually replied that he would travel out to Blue Brush.

Jack showed up after Lockhart spent an anguished time waiting at the homestead which now had a distressingly empty atmosphere and yet, paradoxically, seemed to be haunted by Marcy's lingering presence.

Everything had now turned to ashes: the happy

17

marriage after he and Marcy discovered each other when she was an adventurous girl, teaching school in a raw cattle town; the determination to have a new, settled life and, eventually, children; their early days of homesteading and the dreams of building up a little horse-ranching venture.

All the time, festering within him, was the desire to be actively seeking Dal Colquitt's crew of murderous robbers and wreaking vengeance on Marcy's killer.

After the funeral at Blue Brush's modest little church, Lockhart told his brother-in-law: 'Jack, I want you to attend to disposing of the homestead.'

Jack looked at him, puzzled. 'Just a minute, Dave. Isn't that a bit too drastic? You have to have a home.'

Lockhart shook his head. 'Sell off everything, the property and the animals – the whole shooting-match. You're a man of law, you'll know all about what it entails. Pay up the funeral costs, raise a decent headstone on Marcy's grave from the proceeds and you can bank whatever's left for me after taking whatever fee you figure you're entitled to.'

'Aren't you acting too hastily?' persisted Jack.

'No, I have things to do – a score to settle and there's no time to waste. I'm taking my horse and pretty much only what I stand up in and pulling out,' Lockhart said emphatically.

His brother-in-law looked at him critically. He liked and admired Lockhart and was pleased that

18

his sister had found such a husband in the harsh frontier society that had attracted her talents.

Jack also knew of Lockhart's cavalry and cowpunching background and of his life lived in rugged conditions among rugged men He fully understood the significance of what he was saying and of the Colt revolver, once more holstered at his hip after he had shed it during the funeral for the sake of decency.

Just under his surface, Dave Lockhart had always been a man of action – and, now, he was a deeply embittered one with raw vengeance on his mind.

'There's no doubt about what you're planning, Dave,' said Jack. 'You're simply burning your bridges to go after this fair-haired youngster. I feel the same way about him and I have the same inclination to hunt him down, but we can't take the law into our own hands.'

'That's the lawyer in you talking, Jack,' said Lockhart. 'Tracking a man is a long way out of your line and, anyway, you have a wife and kids to think about. With Marcy gone, I figure I have nothing. And I feel nothing for Blue Brush any more.'

That summed up his empty bleakness. He felt cut off from the Blue Brush community.

The treasured homestead and all the plans he and Marcy had made together meant nothing any more. Lockhart's only desire was to track the kid who killed Marcy even if it took the rest of his life.

A day later he was riding north but with no precise objective other than the Red River and what lay beyond it, for the legends surrounding Dal Colquitt's outlaw bunch adamantly held that the gang had its headquarters somewhere in Indian Territory.

Lockhart was back in character to the ex-cavalry trooper turned rider of the cattle trails, though his equipment lacked the coiled lariat of the cowhand. Behind his Texas saddle, he carried his warsack and bedroll and a couple of panniers containing beef jerky and coarse bread for the trail. The Winchester used by Marcy to inflict the betraying wound on the young Colquitt rider rode in his saddle-scabbard and he vowed it would be used again on Marcy's victim with fatal effect. Anyone noting his trappings and his grim, fixed expression might fairly take him for a bounty hunter.

He rode north into the vast terrain, much of it brush, between the location of his homestead and the long snake of the Red River which separated Texas from Indian Territory, the depository of the tribes driven forcibly from their Southern homelands earlier in the century and now each occupying its own transplanted 'nation'.

Indian Territory, one day to become stable as the state of Oklahoma, held various dangers and attracted a variety of law-dodgers, gunmen, dubious adventurers on the make and the outcasts of a wide section of the Western frontier.

The territory functioned under an uneasy balance of mingled United States law and the tribal laws of the peoples the white men had dubbed 'the

Five Civilized Tribes': the Cherokee, Choctaw, Chickasaw, Creek and Seminole Indians, whose lands in the fertile South had been bargained, negotiated and grabbed out of their hands by a government acting in the interests of moneyed planters and farmers.

Herded by the military on a heartbreaking march and shipped along the Arkansas River by steamboat, the Indian peoples would long, long remember what they came to call the 'Trail of Tears' that took them into the alien and inhospitable landscape in which they were forced to create new settlements.

It was to their credit that the Five Civilized tribes built up their communities, developed farms and townships and retained their dignity in defiance of many white intruders of ill will and villainous intent. Stoically, they survived.

A portion of the upper Red River nudged neighbouring New Mexico Territory. Thereabouts might be found Texans who had a twisted and prejudiced view of their Indian neighbours across the wide river. This was in consequence of the long, bloody and horrifyingly brutal war that had raged between the Comanches and the white settlers, much of which was enacted in that country.

Although the Five Civilized Tribes rebuffed the Comanches when they crossed the Red River and attempted to make allies of them, there were Texans who held bitterly that all Indians, even those from the civilized nations, only became good Indians when dead.

It was towards that harsh, uneasy country that Dave Lockhart was now riding.

The Indian Nations had to be crossed by the Texas trail herds heading for the Kansas railheads and there were numerous well-trafficked crossing points on the river, but the very nature of Dal Colquitt's line of business meant that his gang would hardly enter and leave Texas by any of the most travelled fords of the river. Yet, if they did indeed have some as yet undiscovered hideout in Indian Territory they must have some way over the water used regularly in their bloody excursions into Texas.

With nothing more precise than the belief that Dal Colquitt's bunch had headed for Indian Territory after their raid, Lockhart struck out for the river country, riding much of the time like a mechanical man with vengeful thoughts burning within him. He hardly stopped to think about the folly of a lone-handed attempt to tackle the feared Colquitts even if he did encounter them on this random search.

That he would have such luck in the vast terrain spreading before him was highly questionable but he was spurred his agonized desire for retribution. One man alone he wanted out of the squad of outlaw riders – the young fellow with a head wound, Marcy's killer.

On the first day he rode till dusk, following trails reaching ever riverward. He passed through no settlements and saw no other person before making a trailside night camp and, after a rudimentary supper, unfurling his bedroll and turning in.

In the morning, pressing on with the sun well up, he met a traveller bound the other way. Behind a team drawing a wagon laden with assorted goods, was a grizzled old-timer, obviously a journeying purveyor of merchandise catering to the sparse settlements.

The old man hauled rein on seeing Lockhart's approach and waved a greeting.

'You in need of anything, friend?' he called. 'Soap? Physic for a cough? Medicine for your horse? I have a selection of all kinds of things. All good-quality stuff. Amos Tozer is the name. All the folks in the five counties around here will vouch for me and my wares.'

'All I want is a certain bunch of guys,' said Lockhart. 'More specifically, just one guy. A youngster with a wound to the head and on a calico cayuse.'

He surprised himself by his willingness to talk to this old man, doubtless because this meeting offered relief from the loneliness of his hard travelling.

'Well, now that's a strange thing. Right after I took to the trail this morning, I met up with just such a man. He was aboard a white mare at that,' said the old-timer.

All Lockhart's senses were suddenly alerted. 'You did? Was he alone?'

'Sure. Lonesome as a skunk at a prayer meeting.

23

I saw he had a bandage peeking under the brim of his hat. Surly young fellow. Didn't want to buy anything. Just nodded to me and went on riding.'

'In which direction?'

'Why, just the same way as yourself. He's maybe three hours ahead of you by now,' responded the old man.

'Where do you figure he was going?' enquired Lockhart.

'Squaw Crossing, I guess. That's the only place of any consequence at the end of this trail. Ain't that where you're headed?'

'It is now,' said Lockhart. 'Thanks.' He touched spurs to his mount.

Watching him go, the old man grunted: 'Huh, another tight-fisted joker not willing to part with a cent! I'm plumb sorry I told him about the young fellow with the bandage. I hope he don't catch him whatever grudge there is betwixt 'em!'

Despite the oldster's ill wishes, his information ultimately yielded benefit of a kind to Lockhart. It was the first valuable indication that he had picked up the trail of the killer, if the man was indeed the Colquitt gang member and, if that were the case, he would seem to have cut loose from the rest of the outlaw bunch.

Squaw Crossing was a small town close to a heavily used ford across the river.

Lockhart had never visited it, but knew similar cattle-trail settlements well. Frenziedly bustling when the drive season was in full swing, they were places where all manner of men gathered.

Squaw Crossing was just the kind of place where the fair-haired killer, having for some reason struck out alone and, ducking the law, could seek a place in a trail crew and so disappear into Indian Territory, assured of grub and a certain anonymity among a bunch of beef wranglers.

Now, Lockhart forced his pace northward, riding with much higher expectations.

Close on midday he hit a dim trail that he believed would lead to Squaw Crossing.

He followed it through scrubby brush and tumbled rocks for a couple of miles and was nearing a jumble of rearing boulders around which the trail wound when, abruptly, his horse lifted its head, snorted and gave a quivering whinny.

This reaction strongly suggested a response to the scent of a mare on the wind. Lockhart rode around the rocks and found that they formed a kind of arena in which there was a waterhole, fed by a thin trickle that issued from a mossy natural rockery. It was a perfect travellers' stopover place.

At the further side of the arena, close to piled-up boulders beside the point where the trail continued, there was a young man and a horse, a small calico mare. The man was frozen, interrupted in the act of mounting and Lockhart, riding into view from the rocks on his side of the trail, was startled to see that, with a look of wild-eyed alarm, he was levelling a Colt revolver.

Lockhart saw that, just below his hat brim and

over his right temple, there was a grubby section of a bandage. A lock of fair hair flopped from under the front of the hat.

The fair-haired man's face set in a hard scowl and his mouth became a cruel, thin-lipped gash. It was obvious that he was about to trigger his gun.

It flashed through Lockhart's mind that the man had been alerted by his own animal's whinny, giving him a time to draw his weapon and even as he was grabbing for his gun-butt the other's six-shooter exploded, point blank. Lockhart instinctively dropped his upper body forward over his saddle horn.

In the face of a weapon held at such close proximity, he tried desperately to make himself as small as possible and the closeness of the shot almost deafened him.

He felt a jarring blow to his right cheek and he jerked violently sideways in his saddle. His senses whirled and, dully, he heard the pounding of a horse being speedily ridden away with a jungle of reingbits.

Then he was totally engulfed by a wave of blackness.

CHAPTER TWO

SQUAW CROSSING

Gasping, Lockhart shook his head and, as his vision cleared, he found that he was slumped forward in his saddle, mentally befuddled and with a dull ache in the region of his right cheekbone. Gingerly, he felt the area and encountered only a slight smear of blood. Evidently, whatever had struck him was plainly not a bullet.

There was no sign of the fair-haired man with the bandage covering the vicinity of the temple where Marcy had inflicted a wound on her attacker. Seemingly, he and his calico mare had totally fled the scene.

A scalding anger took hold of Lockhart with the full realization that he had been within mere yards of Marcy's killer and face to face with him, yet he had been robbed of his chance of wreaking a vengeful reckoning upon him.

As he slowly became more lucid he looked around, noting that a large boulder rearing behind the position where he had halted his mount bore a vivid, new-looking scar. He dismounted, searched the ground and spotted a large, sharp-edged shard of rock. He picked it up and found that its edges were clean, indicating that it had been newly chipped off the boulder. It bore a smudge of fresh blood. He reasoned that, despite the devastatingly close range, the gunman had triggered his weapon in panic and the bullet had missed him. It hit the boulder just behind his head and chipped off the chunk of rock.

Though he might have been struck by ricocheting lead, he had been hit by the flying splinter of rock, was rendered briefly unconscious but he had somehow kept in the saddle.

He drew his Colt and scouted the site, wary of the man's still being somewhere in the surrounding rocks. He saw no sign of him and reasoned that he had ridden off, probably from where the trail snaked away in the direction of Squaw Crossing.

'If he's the guy I'm looking for and it looks as if he is, why did he shoot?' he said aloud to his horse. 'He doesn't know me from Adam and doesn't know I'm after him. And where's the rest of Colquitt's bunch? Can the whole crew be somewhere around here or has that joker cut loose from them for some reason? Has he vamoosed completely? Is he running around this wild country and still a danger

28

or has he gone on into Squaw Crossing?'

He made a close inspection of the surroundings of the waterhole, and saw recent tracks of only one pair of boots, one deposit of recent horse droppings and no discarded cigarette butts which would tell the tale of a group of men making a substantial stopover there.

'He was on his lonesome. There's no doubt of it.' he murmured as he let his horse drink.

He slaked his own thirst, splashed water on his aching cheekbone and replenished his canteen, pondering the mystery of why the man, plainly the one he sought, was not with the rest of the Colquitt gang.

He considered the sky and saw that dusk would soon be gathering. He must hasten to Squaw Crossing and seek some rest for himself and his horse as well as whatever information he might chance on there, assuming he did not encounter either his fair-haired quarry or the rest of Dal Colquitt's marauders somewhere along the way.

With the uneasy feeling that he might run into them anywhere along these dim and obscure trails, he pressed on. He did not encounter anyone and, as shadows lengthened, he reached Squaw Crossing, a town famed as a trail-herd stopover but to which he was a stranger, never having accompanied a herd through it in his trail-driving days.

Situated close to a reasonably easy ford over the Red River into the Indian Nations used by periodic herds, Squaw Crossing needed a strong and vigilant town marshal, which it had in the doughty person of Bill Ritter.

A veteran of various cattle and mining towns, Ritter might no longer be young but his stocky body was still energetic. He had a craggy, weather-burned face, a white longhorn moustache, undimmed eyes and a razor-sharp intellect.

Ritter stood on the plankwalk outside his office in the company of a tall man who wore the encircled star of the Texas Rangers on his military-style shirt.

'What do you make of this fellow, Captain Thewlis?' he asked, nodding to indicate the rider progressing in their direction over the rutted dust of the town's single street.

Both men scrunched their eyes against the still strong glare of the lowering late-afternoon sun.

They took in the appearance of the approaching stranger with the sharply critical scrutiny of veteran lawmen.

He was of slim and wiry build and the straight-backed style of his seat suggested cavalry experience. Under his wide hat-brim, his face had an embittered hardness. His mount carried saddle-panniers, betokening long horseback journeying. Such handy panniers were part of Texas Ranger equipment but Thewlis knew that this was no Ranger.

Ritter and the Ranger captain strode off the plankwalk to meet the rider who pulled rein when he saw them approaching and sat still, stolidly awaiting them.

'I think I know his breed and he'll bear investigating,' said Captain Fred Thewlis suspiciously. Without any preliminaries, he called: 'Are you some kind of bounty hunter, mister?' All the fierce animosity of the Texas Rangers towards freelance trackers, bounty hunters and vigilantes was in his voice and it irked Lockhart.

'No,' he responded flatly.

'I'm Bill Ritter, town marshal here,' interjected Ritter. 'Who're you?'

'I'm just a simple citizen,' responded Lockhart. 'My name's Dave Lockhart, from out Blue Brush way.'

The lawmen eyed him critically, checking his appearance against the portraits and descriptions of wanted owlhooters stored in their brains. They noted the angry-looking recent weal on his right cheek. A man recently in trouble, both thought.

'Lockhart', said the Ranger officer. 'I know that name. You're the homesteader whose wife was killed by the Colquitt bunch. Reports of it reached every Ranger station in the state. Well, I have some good news for you, Mr Lockhart. The Colquitt gang is wiped out. They were cornered and finished off in a shoot-out with a squad of Rangers leading a citizens' posse just outside Rock City, a few miles along the river. I was there to enjoy it. It was as good a day's work as the Texas Rangers ever did, even if we never did find where their hideout was located.'

There was a ring of pompous self-congratulation about his words. He sounded like the victor of some historic field of battle.

'Wiped out? All of 'em?' asked Lockhart with a gasp.

'Yeah. They're all over and done with – including Dal Colquitt himself, and we've been after him for years.'

'I know it,' said Lockhart with biting bitterness. 'Too bad your Rangers didn't get that bunch before they committed murder at my place, but at least the Rock City people had the guts to set up a posse. That's more than the Blue Brush folks did.'

'Rock City had a powerful motive. Colquitt's gang robbed the town bank a couple of years ago and killed a teller,' said Thewlis. 'I'll admit we were helped. The Rangers received an anonymous note in the mails saying another raid was planned so we were prepared. Looks like the Colquitts had a traitor among 'em. The town celebrated, propping the corpses of Colquitt and his crew on boards outside the undertaker's parlour and taking photographs.'

'Was one a young fellow – a kid with fair hair with a recent head injury?'

The Ranger reflected for a moment. 'No, I can't say any could be called young. All were pretty well along in years. There was no kid.'

'Then you didn't get the whole bunch,' said Lockhart testily. 'There was a kid with fair hair in the raid on my place and I'm out to get him. He

32

killed my wife and he's on the loose. I had a run-in with him at the waterhole back yonder. He took a shot at me then vamoosed. I figure he headed this way.'

'Hold hard,' said Thewlis. 'You say you're out to get him. The Rangers don't much care for gents who take the law into their own hands, Mr Lockhart.'

'Maybe that's because damn few of them ever came home to find their wives dying of gunshot wounds,' growled Lockhart bitterly.

'If this fellow's on the loose, we haven't seen him in Squaw Crossing,' said Marshal Ritter. 'I have two good deputies and we keep a tight eye on strangers who come through. If he's left over from Colquitt's crew, he'd be wise to keep away.'

Marshal Ritter paused, fixed Lockhart with a steady gaze and added: 'I'll give you a warning while I'm at it. I don't doubt you're an upright citizen and you have an understandable grudge. I sympathize with you, but if you do spot him here in my bailiwick, leave the law enforcement to me and my deputies.'

'And the whole of this state is the jurisdiction of the Texas Rangers,' cautioned Captain Thewlis in his pompous, self-important way.

He eyed Lockhart in a scarcely friendly fashion and emphasized his point. 'So just watch your step so long as you're on this side of the Red River. A young fellow, fair-haired and with a head wound, you say. I'll remember that and circulate it around the Ranger companies – just in case he really exists.'

Lockhart scowled, thinking that the Ranger was all but calling him a liar. The officer's whole attitude implied smug conviction that the career of Colquitt's outfit was ended by the action of the Rangers and their citizen allies and that no gang member could have slipped the net. Lockhart seethed inwardly.

Holding down his resentment, he answered defiantly: 'He exists, all right, and nothing will stop me from catching up with him whatever side of the river he's on.'

Thewlis grunted: 'I'll allow you've suffered a cruel blow, Mr Lockhart, but don't go risking a Texas hangrope. The law might be loosened up among the Indians on yonder side of the river but it's plumb tight here in Texas, as you should know.'

Of the two lawmen, Marshal Ritter seemed the more friendly and he demonstrated his goodwill by saying: 'That's a sore-looking cut on your cheek, Mr Lockhart. I wouldn't want you to think we don't treat visitors right in Squaw Crossing. Ride up to my office and you can clean it up and I'll give you a strip of court plaster for it.'

With Thewlis and Ritter walking one on either side of his horse, Lockhart rode on towards the solidly constructed building bearing the sign of the town marshal's office.

A rangy roan was hitched outside. Its trappings included the light panniers which were customary Texas Ranger trail equipment.

Addressing Squaw Crossing's lawman, Captain Thewlis said: 'I'll be moving on, Bill. My respects to Miss Ritter.' He strode off towards the hitched animal, then, turning in mid-stride, called back sternly: 'Remember, Lockhart, the Rangers don't care for gents who take the law into their own hands.'

Marshal Ritter smiled. 'Just like Fred Thewlis to insist on the last word. He's a good man at his job but he's mighty stiff-necked about the reputation of the Rangers. He was just passing through to give me word about the Colquitt gang. You happened along at the right time to hear the news.'

At the hitchrack Lockhart dismounted and took in Squaw Crossing's huddle of typical frontier buildings, now touched by the rose and gold of the descending sun. Right across from the town marshal's premises he saw a restaurant, a gunsmith, a barber, a saddlemaker and, incongruously among such neighbours, a store whose frontage bore the legend: HELENE, Gowns and Dresses.

There was also a newspaper office, a sure sign of a town with some energy. On the whole, he liked the look of Squaw Crossing. Doubtless because of its position on the trail-driving route and its importance on account of the ford, it had a good deal more fire in its belly than sleepy Blue Brush.

Further along the street stood the usual garish trail-town saloon-cum-dancehall.

There were also a wide-doored livery stable and a taller building of substantial clapboard with the very

35

welcome label: HOTEL.

They entered the town marshal's office, a large room with the ceiling-to-floor barred gates of a couple of unoccupied cells at its further end and a display of reward posters.

Nearer the door there was a big desk and, sitting behind it was a woman, perhaps in her late twenties with a strikingly good-looking and intelligent face framed by neatly braided auburn hair. Only her upper body was visible, clad in a brocaded shirtwaist rather more stylish than was usual on the frontier.

Surprised by her presence, Lockhart touched the brim of his hat and said: 'Marshal Ritter told me he had two good deputies. I sure didn't expect to find that at least one is a lady.'

She tossed her head back and gave an attractive peal of laughter. Suddenly, Marcy came into Lockhart's mind. This woman's laughter was wholly unlike Marcy's, but her spontaneous reaction of merriment was a haunting reminder of the way his wife responded when something struck her as humorous.

'I'm not a deputy,' she said pleasantly. 'I just come over once in a while to give Dad a hand with his paperwork. He says my handwriting is more readable than his scrawl. That's my place across the street – Helene's the dressmaker's shop. The extra "e" at the end of the name is to let the local ladies feel they're getting some French style with their fashions.'

'This is Helen, my daughter,' said the lawman. 'Helen, this is Dave Lockhart, the homesteader from over Blue Brush way. His wife was a victim of Dal Colquitt's robbers. They shot her when they raided their homestead.'

His daughter suddenly became serious and sympathy came into her hazel eyes. It was mingled with something else – a hard to define quality that implied she had a particular understanding of another's plight. With some shocked guilt, he found that this young woman stirred feelings in him he had not known since he first set eyes on Marcy.

'Oh, I'm sorry,' she said quietly. 'Bob McCourt, who runs our local paper, had the story, or as much as he could gather from his sources. It said the evidence was that she stood off the Colquitts to defend your home. She must have been a very brave woman.'

'She was,' said Lockhart, 'and to my shame, I wasn't there when she needed me.'

'The Colquitts are finished,' Ritter informed his daughter. 'The whole outfit was dispatched by the Rangers and a posse near Rock City.'

'Not quite the whole lot,' corrected Lockhart. 'One is loose and he's somewhere in this river country. He's the one who killed my wife.'

'And you're looking for him,' said Helen with her strangely knowing and sympathetic eyes fixed on him. 'You have the look of a hunter, Mr Lockhart.'

'He's looking for him, all right,' confirmed her father. 'Captain Thewlis and I have been cautioning

37

him about running foul of the law while he's about it.'

Marshal Ritter paused for a moment, looked at Lockwood with his head on one side like a man considering the qualities of a horse, smiled wryly and added: 'I figure I can evaluate a man, and everything about Mr Lockhart suggests he's not easily deterred, even by people so formidable as Captain Thewlis and myself. He has a stubborn bearing and I noted that sits his saddle like a former horse soldier. Am I right?'

'I was a corporal in General Steedman's command. I was with him in the campaign against the Apaches in Scorched Flats, Arizona,' admitted Lockhart, startled by the acuteness of the lawman's perception.

'I knew it.' Marshal Ritter nodded. 'I reckon that is the kind of background to make a gent like you likely to search every last mile of the Red River, even though it runs all the way down to the Mississippi. Well, remember to watch your step. Helen, don't we have some court plaster somewhere about the place so our guest can dress that cut on his face?'

Helen Ritter searched a desk drawer. 'It's in here,' she said and she handed a strip of surgical plaster across to Lockhart. Then she passed him a lace-edged and distinctly feminine handkerchief. It brought Marcy vividly to mind again. She had appreciated ladylike finery. He thought with a pang of guilt that he never eased her hard working homestead life with anything like enough of it, but

38

she never once complained. 'There's a sink and pump over in the corner. You can clean up there,' said Helen.

Lockhart moved over to the sink and began to clean up the wound with water. Leaning against a wall that bore a large-scale map of a wide section of northern Texas, Marshal Ritter began to fill a big corncob pipe, then lit it leisurely.

'I always had a feeling that the Colquitts crossed into Texas somewhere north-west of here,' he observed. 'It's tangled country out that way, within reach of the Staked Plains of New Mexico, spreading into Texas. It's sparsely populated up that way.'

Ritter stabbed at a point on the river region on the map with the stem of his pipe and added: 'Nobody ever saw them cross the river, either coming or going, but the pattern of their actions, never ranging too far south or west from this general region, suggests they have some affinity with it. Curiously enough, they never raided Squaw Crossing, though we have a fat little bank. It could be a prime target after a herd has been driven through.'

'Maybe that's because they know the quality of the town marshal and the two deputies you were telling me about,' commented Lockhart.

Marshal Ritter prodded the map with his pipe-stem again, emphasizing the portion of the Red River landscape where no settlements were marked. 'Suppose the fellow you tangled with back yonder really was the gent you're looking for and suppose he was for some reason following the travel pattern of Colquitt's crew, he could be heading for this region right here. I've always had a hunch that the Colquitt gang's headquarters were located somewhere about there.'

'Maybe so,' said Lockhart thoughtfully as he patted the strip of plaster over the cut on his face.

He reflected that, for one who wished to restrain his, Lockhart's, vengeful sentiments, the veteran lawman was being unusually helpful. He looked out of the open door of the office. The rapidly darkening street made him feel heavily weary and he realized how long it was since he had had any sleep. He yearned for rest yet, all the time, he was nagged by the awareness that his chances of catching up with his fair-haired quarry were slipping away.

The man had obviously avoided Squaw Crossing and might already have had time to quit Texas for Indian Territory, or maybe its neighbouring Oklahoma Territory. Yet Lockhart knew he must capitulate to his fatigue. The hours in the saddle on top of the residue of shock and anxiety after Marcy's death were all taking their toll on his energy and mental strength.

'I'm obliged to you for your kindness,' he told Ritter and his daughter. 'I figure I'll go in search of a meal and a bed in the hotel.'

'Well, both the restaurant and hotel are of reasonable quality if not luxurious,' said Marshal Ritter.

Lockhart nodded to the lawman, touched his hat brim to his daughter and strode to the door.

From behind the desk, Helen Ritter could see his progress as he led his horse from the hitchrack across the shadowed and rutted width of the street towards the livery stable.

'He's a determined man, Dad,' she said gravely. 'Mighty determined and mighty embittered and, as for you, you puzzle me. You preach about not wanting lawlessness and gunplay, yet, with your theories about where he might find his man, and pinpointing the map, you were almost encouraging him to perpetrate violence.'

'Sure,' said her father. 'Maybe I was a mite carried away but it's plain to me that a man of his calibre won't quit searching for his wife's killer even if it leads to his own death by gunplay or brings him to the gallows.'

Helen shuddered. 'I wouldn't want that to happen to him. You can see right off he's too good a man to go courting a violent and miserable death.'

With a pang in his heart, Marshal Bill Ritter noted the tenderness in his daughter's face and the catch in her voice as she spoke.

'Yes, but he's a man who'll push his luck just because he is a decent man who's thirsting for justice,' he rumbled. 'I feel for him because if the same thing had happened to your poor late mother as happened to his wife when I was his age, I'd be just as bitter and just as determined to hand out my

41

own brand of justice – from a gun barrel! For all the authority vested in my lawman's star, maybe I'm just too blamed old to cure myself of a yearning for frontier justice.'

CHAPTER THREE

HELEN

After seeing his horse settled at the livery stable with clean straw and fodder, Lockhart found that Squaw Crossing's restaurant and hotel were indeed of reasonable quality and he slept soundly, his last tangled waking thoughts being of Ritter's pointed hint suggesting the western region of the Red River as the focus of his search and reminding him of the urgency of locating his quarry. If the wound to the young man's temple healed, he cast off that distinguishing strip of bandage and his fair locks were concealed by his hat, the man would be all the harder to identify.

In the morning, greatly refreshed, cleaned and shaved, Lockhart paid his hotel bill and stepped out into the crisp air. His mind was on breakfast, after which he intended to lose no time in riding towards the western region of the Red River.

The town was slowly awakening. To reach the eating-house, he had to pass Helen Ritter's dressmaking shop. Poised in its window, a couple of dummy female figures in smart costumes and florally decorated millinery brought Marcy back to mind again. He thought how elegant she would have looked in such finery and of how he had never provided it for her, not because of parsimony but simply through thoughtlessness. Biting his lip, he reflected that he had never fully deserved Marcy, and never valued her enough.

Glancing beyond the mannequins in the window, he saw that Helen Ritter was already astir, sitting behind a long counter and handling some lengths of material. She looked up, spotted him, smiled and beckoned him to enter.

Hesitantly, he went into the premises and found that she was alone. There was a tempting tang in the air and he saw a bubbling coffee pot set on a spirit stove on a table in one corner.

'Good morning,' Helen greeted. 'Sleep well? Want an early coffee? I keep some ready for my ladies. They mostly have to travel in from ranches and homesteads and they appreciate a cup and a chat when they arrive – and it's a good business move.'

Lockhart accepted the unexpected offer with thanks, then Helen Ritter's early-morning breeziness melted and she considered him with the particular quality of sympathy that seemed all her own.

'You know, Dave – I can call you Dave, can't I? I thought about you a lot last night,' she said quietly. 'I thought of how hurt and angry you must be. But don't let it eat at you. Bitterness and resentment are destructive. I didn't know your wife but I'd have been proud to. I know she was courageous and not scared to face up to the odds even when they were dead against her. She was surely a woman of real value. I'll bet she wouldn't want her man to be all embittered inside because of something that, in the end, he couldn't help. That wasn't the man she married. It's a sure thing that she'd want her man to be the man she married. Keep the bitterness at bay.'

Lockhart twisted his mouth, showing some resentment. 'That's easily said by someone like you, Helen. This might be a trail town and some might see it as half-civilized but I reckon you've been fortunate enough to live a pretty genteel life here with your dressmaking and all. Maybe I can be bold enough to doubt if you were ever had real cause for bitterness.'

Helen gave him an intriguing half-smile with her eyebrows raised almost amusedly.

'Meaning I'm in no position to lecture you? Well, I suppose you're right—' She broke off abruptly and said: 'Hey, that coffee pot is about to boil over! It's sometimes tricky. I'll handle it.'

She bent down from her seat to collect something from under the counter. Lockhart's eyes widened and he felt an almost physical blow on seeing that it was a crutch. He realized that, hitherto, he had only ever seen Helen Ritter when she was seated and never standing or walking.

She came around from behind the counter with the crutch under her right arm, walking quickly in an expertly controlled and graceful way, making for the table and its coffee pot. Her long skirt with its fashionable bustle concealed any evidence of why she needed the crutch.

Acutely embarrassed, Lockhart wished the floorboards would open and swallow him up and, in a flustered mumble, he offered: 'I'm sorry.'

She looked at him from where she was pouring coffee with her left hand.

'About what?' she asked, then his discomfiture registered with her and she slapped the crutch with her right hand and said: 'Oh, about Peggy here? I guess this is the first time you've seen her. She's usually out of sight under my counter or under Dad's desk. I forget I have her most of the time. She's pretty much part of me by now. There's nothing to be sorry about.'

'I'm sorry about saying you could hardly have cause for bitterness. I was talking plumb out of turn,' he muttered.

She regarded him in her deep way and he felt a quiet rapport growing between them in spite of his gaffe.

Holding out a cup of coffee, she said soberly: 'I'd have figured you had enough experience of the world to know that everyone suffers some blows in life. Nobody escapes them and we all have to recover from a kick in the teeth at some time.'

She poured herself some coffee, added cream, took a sip, looked quizzically at Lockhart, then eased his embarrassment by saying with a mischievous smile: 'Well, do I continue philosophizing or do you want to hear why I need Peggy's help? Her name stands for "peg-leg", by the way. Oh, I have the usual number of legs but one doesn't work properly. I was run over by an ore wagon when I was ten and Dad was a deputy in a mining town in New Mexico. My foot was badly crushed and the only medical man around was a drunk. His attempts at surgery made things worse. I haven't been able to walk on the foot since and I never shall as long as I live.'

She saw concern in his face, countered it with another smile. 'As a matter of fact, a crutch can be a mighty handy accessory for a lady in a cowtown. I reckon you'll know the kind of gent who shows up here when the trail herds are passing through. They'll be here any day now when the first of the season's drives arrives – cowhands blowing their last spare dollar on liquor before crossing into Indian Territory and going up the long trail. Even a town marshal's daughter with one useable foot can encounter pests. You'd be astonished at the civilizing effects of a sharp crack with Peggy over a wrangler's knee when he least expects it.'

For the first time, she saw him smile; his look of the embittered hunter melted.

'You'd be justified in giving me some of that treatment,' he said. 'You're pretty remarkable. Pretty tolerant, too, when it comes to a fellow who hands out what I reckon is called an uninformed opinion.'

'You might say pretty lucky, as well,' she said modestly. 'My mother died five years ago. She was a skilled dressmaker and taught me the trade and some business sense. We opened this place between us and it's doing well. I feel I'm a deal more fortunate than many a woman.'

Lockhart stood facing her, drinking his coffee and a silence fell between them. Her attractive eyes considered him with that almost disturbing depth of understanding, then she said calmly: 'You're a good man, Dave Lockhart, and I know that what my father said last night will send you chasing all along the river. Just don't get hurt.'

He considered her slim, straight figure. Her crutch did indeed appear a mere accessory rather than an indication of physical impairment. Moreover, he could see it as a badge of her courage. He drained his cup and placed it on the nearby counter.

He felt a lump rise in his throat as he told her: 'You said you'd have been proud to have known Marcy. Well, she would sure enough be proud to have known you.'

He turned for the door. When just about to open it, he halted and turned.

'Your father said he had suspicions about the

country up yonder on the fringe of the Staked Plains. Have you any idea of the specific location he meant?' he asked.

'Probably the Smoke Canyon and Salt Pass region of the river,' she answered. 'I'm told Salt Pass is a wild town on the Indian Territory side and the canyon is on the Texas side. The whole location has had a bad reputation since the days when the Comanche raided over that way. There's a lot of superstition surrounding it.' Then her face clouded and she looked guilty, as if she could have bitten out her tongue.

'Smoke Canyon and Salt Pass,' he said with a nod. 'Thanks.'

'Maybe I shouldn't have told you that,' said Helen hesitantly. 'I hear Salt Pass attracts riff-raff from all parts of Texas, the Indian Nations and New Mexico. Anyway, going there could be just as much a wild-goose chase as coming here.'

Lockhart looked at her levelly. She saw his eyes soften and the hint of a smile quirk his lips. 'Coming to Squaw Crossing was no wild-goose chase, Helen,' he said, lifting his hat.

He left the shop and strode with ringing spurs along the plankwalk towards the eating-house for breakfast. With her graceful management of her crutch, Helen swung swiftly towards the window and watched him go. She saw determination in his stride and noted the businesslike way he packed his revolver. The brief, sympathetic softening of his face had given way to the look of the hunter once more, but she was aware that that was no more than a veneer, covering finer feelings within the man.

Helen Ritter, you're every kind of fool! she admonished herself inwardly. 'Too bad you don't have two good legs. You could give yourself a well-deserved kick!' she added aloud. 'Why did you have to pinpoint the Smoke Canyon country? Maybe you've sent him headlong into danger.'

The memory of her father's words about Lockhart's quest leading him to death by bullets or even to the gallows came to her and, again, she shuddered.

Then she added, still aloud: 'But perhaps you're more your old town-taming father's daughter than you ever knew. Maybe the manner of Dave Lockhart's wife's murder is bringing out his thirst for frontier justice in you, too!"

CHAPTER FOUR

TROUBLE ON
THE TRAIL

Putting horseback miles between himself and Squaw Crossing, Dave Lockhart now and again had the deterring thought that he might be simply chasing the wind. His only compass was Marshal Bill Ritter's feeling that the fair-haired youngster's bypassing of Squaw Crossing might indicate that he was heading for what the lawman felt was the home base of the Colquitts, and his only guidance as to destination was Helen's pinpointing of Salt Pass. Thoughts of quitting, however, soon raised his burning thirst to avenge Marcy's death, forcing him to press onward, following these, his only semblances of guidance.

Wherever the kid was, he'd find him even if he searched the whole of the earth.

He rode through largely uninhabited and flat

country with the Red River to the north, following a trail that was vague in parts and seemingly little travelled. The terrain changed slightly towards the end of his first day of travel, becoming more rocky and tangled. With the first shades of night he found a rock-guarded pool of clear water. It was the ideal place for a night camp with water and clumps of grass to provide his horse with graze.

He dismounted, divested his mount of his saddle, bedroll and panniers, led the animal to the pool and, after it drank, tethered it to a stout clump of brush. Then he prepared to settle for the night, building a fire and laying out his sleeping gear. After a meagre supper of coffee and black bread he slept dreamlessly and woke with first light feeling refreshed.

He rekindled the glowing remains of the fire with fresh brushwood and set about preparing coffee. As the sun began to climb in the azure sky, he had the fire going well and his first helping of coffee was quickly prepared and consumed.

As he chewed jerky, he replenished the pot and returned it to the fire for reheating. Squatting by the fire, he froze at the sound of approaching horses. He looked around and saw two riders appear out of the haze of early sunlight. One was tall, the other shorter and somewhat stooped in the saddle. Their range garb was well-worn and they wore heavy shell belts at their waists. The butt of a Navy Colt was visible in the holster of one and his companion sported a Smith & Wesson.

Riders and mounts were gaunt, marked by wearisome travelling, and the men's faces were hard-bitten. Their whole demeanour, from their slumped way of riding to their general slovenliness, was sufficient to spark caution in a beholder.

Lockwood eyed them suspiciously as they drew rein. They might be cowhands but, remembering Helen's description of Salt Pass, yonder along the trail, as a gathering place for riff-raff, they looked like dubious saddle tramps and might easily be owlhooters on the dodge.

'Coffee smells good,' called the taller man, licking his lips.

'Sure,' responded Lockhart. Then, impelled by the traditions of the trail, he added:

'Care to join me?'

'That's mighty civilized of you,' said the bigger man.

'Mighty civilized,' echoed the shorter one in a throaty growl.

The strangers dismounted, led their animals to the stream, left them drinking noisily, then walked towards Lockhart.

'You a Ranger?' asked the short one with a certain narrowing of the eyes. The tone of his voice conveyed a wariness of Texas Rangers.

'No, I'm no Ranger.'

The short one nodded towards Lockhart's tethered mount. 'Them panniers on your cayuse seem the same as Rangers carry. That's what made me ask.'

'I just happen to have picked them up cheap years ago and they're useful,' said Lockhart in a seemingly easy and conversational way.

He saw the short man exchange a fleeting but significantly dangerous glance with his trail partner and he immediately regretted imparting the information that he was not a Texas Ranger. Though he was without a badge, in present company it might have been safer to pretend to be one.

This pair could easily be out to kill him and rob him, something they would hesitate to do if he was a Ranger, for his murder would put the full fury of Ranger vengeance on their tails. The style of this pair put Lockhart fully on the alert. One way or another, he was going to have trouble with them.

'Not a Ranger, huh?' croaked the short one. 'Are you maybe a friend of Dirksen, on the way to Salt Pass to meet up with him?' This was asked in a furtive and cautious way.

'No. Who's Dirksen? I can't say I know of him,' replied Lockhart.

'Oh, he's just a guy. It don't make no never mind no ways.'

'We're just out of Squaw Crossing, a mite back along the trail,' said the tall man, conversationally and obviously eager to change the subject. He strode up to where Lockhart squatted near the fire and stood over him, trying to look casual.

'There's a trail herd going through Squaw Crossing,' he said. 'We figured we'd get took on for the drive. Not a chance, though. No hands wanted.'

'Tough luck,' sympathized Lockhart. He glanced towards the new arrivals' horses by the water and a detail he had missed earlier registered – neither animal had the cattleman's customary coiled lariat riding at the fore of its saddle. The pair were not working cow wranglers and the yarn about seeking jobs on the drive was a lie aimed at disarming him.

Lockhart made a show of giving his attention to the coffee pot but he watched the tall man with the tail of his eye and, with alarm stabbing at his innards, he saw his right hand drop towards the Navy Colt at his shell belt.

Lockhart grabbed the handle of the pot, jerked up to a standing position and, at the same time, slung the whole volume of scalding coffee full into the man's face.

The man staggered back with a screech that ended in gurgling sobs of agony. He whirled around in a grotesque, drunken dance with both hands clapped to his face.

His short companion, standing only yards away, froze and was transfixed for a moment. Then, his eyes widened and his face worked into an astonished mask.

He clawed his Smith & Wesson out of its holster. The instant he levelled it at Lockhart, he fired but Lockhart hurled himself to one side. He felt the slug *whang* past him, fanning his face, and he hit the ground on his back.

He rolled, fumbling for his six-gun and managed

to haul it free of its leather. As the short man loomed over him with a menacingly flourished weapon, he fired upwards.

The short man gave a sharp, agonized yelp, dropped like a log and lay still.

Lockhart stood up to find that the tall man had ceased his agonized dancing to some degree. His hat was off and his Navy Colt weapon was lying on the ground. In a blind fury, he staggered forward, with one hand clutching his face. With the other, he flailed a balled fist in Lockhart's direction. Fighting for breath, Lockhart ducked the fist, brought his gun barrel down on the bare head of his attacker and felled him.

Striving to overcome the effects of shock and his physical efforts, Lockhart surveyed the scene.

The short man was stone dead, drilled through the middle of the forehead. His companion was unconscious, lying on his back with his face showing a scarlet weal caused by the hot coffee.

Lockhart held down flutters of panic. He had killed a man. On this side of the Red River, he would have the Texas Rangers and the federal marshals on his track when it came to light. He could fairly claim self-defence, though he had no witness other than the dead man's companion who hardly counted.

In a chilling moment, he realized that the hangman's rope loomed in his future.

Looking at the pair now, he saw plainly that they were law-dodgers for sure, gaunt, ill-fed and doubtless short of resources. They had approached his encampment fully intent on robbing him, possibly after merely beating him, but the memory of the tall man's decisive drawing of his gun as Lockhart squatted at the fire suggested a more deadly intent from the outset.

If this pair had indeed passed through Squaw Crossing where, according to them, the first of the season's trail herds had arrived, it was likely that vigilant Marshal Bill Ritter and his deputies had noted them. Possibly they were not known to the law and could not be held, but their general demeanour was likely to arouse the suspicions of astute law officers. Possibly Ritter and his deputies could give testimony in Lockhart's favour if the law did descend on him, but it was a slim chance.

Lockhart knew he must get clear of this place as quickly as possible. The tall man was already groaning and stirring. Soon he would be conscious and, so far as Lockhart was concerned, he could deal with the aftermath of the brawl as best he could after Lockhart hastened from the scene. Lockhart reasoned that he was most unlikely to go in search of the law.

Now Lockhart's immediate priority was to get out of Texas and across the river into Indian Territory as quickly as he could make tracks. He gathered up his bedroll, saddled his horse, loaded bedroll and panniers and departed.

As he set off from the campsite at a smart jog, he heard the tall man spluttering curses, obviously surfacing from his unconscious state.

Intent on riding clear of Texas law, Lockhart kept up a steady pace and, as his tangled thoughts became more rational, he remembered the shorter man's question concerning a rendezvous with someone in Salt Pass. What was the name he mentioned? It came to him – Dirksen.

The indications were that the two owlhooters were themselves on the way to meet this Dirksen and that they had thought at first that he was one of their own kind on a similar errand.

In that case, the man he left at the campsite might well continue the journey in his wake. That prompted a sobering thought. At the time, it had seemed a good idea to leave everything at the campsite as it was and depart fast, but the unconscious man had been left in possession of his own handgun, that of his dead companion and two Henry rifles as well as his dead partner's horse.

There was every danger that, once he recovered his wits sufficiently, he might well follow Lockhart and attempt to backshoot him as soon as he was within sight of him. Now, Lockhart rode with an eye to his backtrail.

The sun rode high, crossed its zenith and the afternoon was passed on a trail barren and unpeopled. This section of the river country appeared to offer no enticement to settlers. His frequent checks of the trail at his back revealed no sign of dust to suggest that he was being followed.

At early dusk he found a trail branching off

towards the bottomlands of the Red River. Beside it a slanted finger-post bore, in crudely written letters, the words: Salt Pass.

'A guide for all that riff-raff,' muttered Lockhart, 'though it don't seem as if any are making the pilgrimage right now.'

The trail followed downwardly slanting land and the smell and sound of the River strengthened. Suddenly, he came to the water, flowing where the trail passed over what was obviously a shallow ford.

The gathering dusk was pierced by blotches of light sparkling on the far side of the river and a faint suggestion of music drifted over the water.

'Looks like we're at the gates of Salt Pass,' he said to his mount as he pulled rein. He dismounted to stretch his legs. His back trail still revealed no indication of a pursuer and, after his horse had drunk at the river, he remounted and crossed the ford.

The trail continued for a short distance from the crossing. Then, when he rounded a spur of land, Lockhart found he was at the head of the town's single street. Its broad width spliced a huddle of buildings as nondescript and ugly as any on the frontier.

Under the deepening mantle dusk, Salt Pass looked as uninviting as he had imagined from Helen Ritter's description of it as a gathering place for assorted undesirables. Splashes of dim yellow lamplight picked out windows and showed scatterings of shadowed humanity moving around the plankwalks. All appeared to have a furtiveness that was of a piece with the overriding spirit of furtiveness that seemed to possess the place.

Lockhart sniffed the air and commented to his mount: 'I recollect something from Scripture about no mean city but it's a fair bet Salt Pass can't make any such proud claim. It looks – and smells – meaner than any place I ever saw.'

On the very edge of town, he spotted what was obviously a saloon. It was a squat building of weathered clapboard from whence issued a buzz of voices mingled with the tortured clinking of a ill-tuned piano. Yellow lamplight bloomed from its grimy windows and splashed across its scuffed plank gallery before which an assortment of horses and wagons were hitched at two racks.

Nearing the saloon, he saw three riders coming from the opposite direction.

They were wide-hatted and heavily garbed, riding at a walk as if they had made a long journeying. Their demeanour might cause a man to toss a coin on the question of what they were but they had the suspicious look of outlaws, of the same brotherhood as the pair who had tried to jump him on the trail.

They reached the saloon, dismounted, hitched their animals, clomped up the couple of plank steps to the gallery and passed through the batwings.

The swinging doors let out intermittent flashes of brighter light, vividly illuminating one of the horses already hitched at the rack before the arrival of the trio – a sturdy little calico mare!

The sight caused Lockhart to knee his animal's ribs to speed his approach.

He told himself that the world held more than one calico mare, but this one was familiar, strongly resembling the animal he had seen with the man at the waterhole before he reached Squaw Crossing, though he had glimpsed the animal only briefly.

He reached the front of the saloon, swung out of his saddle and went up to the line of hitched animals. He looked closely at the head of the mare. She had a white blaze across the front of her face as, so far as he remembered, had the animal of the man he encountered at the waterhole. Still he could not be sure. Marcy's fair-haired killer might be in the saloon – or the calico mare might be a wholly false lead.

He looped his reins over the rack and mounted the steps, with no hard plan of action but with an ungovernable impulsiveness prodded by rising fury at the prospect of meeting up with Marcy's killer again. He nudged his Colt loose in its holster and breasted the batwings.

He entered an atmosphere fogged by pungent tobacco smoke and dinning with an amalgam of voices, clinking glasses and flat piano music.

What must have been the greater part of the population of Salt Pass seemed to be drinking and gaming in the place. To judge from appearances, Helen Ritter was wholly correct in saying that this town gathered assorted riffraff. Gun-hung gentry lined the long bar, sat at tables, tossing back liquor or handling cards, while a cluster of hopefuls took their chances at the whirling chuckaluck wheel in a far corner.

A derby-hatted 'musician' hammered a rickety piano and the woeful effects of his labours fought to override the raucous babble of speech and harsh laughter.

Lockhart squinted through the drifting levels of acrid smoke. At a table only a short distance away he saw the three men who had entered shortly before. They were standing around a seated man with whom they were in deep, grim-faced conversation.

He looked young, with his hat shoved back on his head – revealing a cowlick of fair hair and a grubby, blood-marked bandage stretched over his brow.

Gritting his teeth against the anger that surged up in him like a physical wave, Lockhart fought down the almost insane instinct to swoop on Marcy's killer and strangle him with his bare hands. He realized that there was nothing he could do to avenge his wife here, in this place, crammed with dangerous-looking humanity. He realized that the fair-haired man had obtained a good look at him when they had run into each other before Lockhart reached Squaw Crossing. His sight only had to waver from his hard case companions and he would spot Lockhart.

Recognition might lead to dangerous play in which he would surely be backed by his coterie of pistol-heavy henchmen.

Ducking behind a nearby pillar, Lockhart kept

his back to the group at the table and made for the bar. He slipped behind the broad back of a big man who was part of a noisy group, conversing and cackling with laughter. In that position, he was shielded from the view of the men at the table but, with his hat-brim pulled down and his head slightly twisted, he could keep them under observation.

He ordered a beer as an excuse to station himself at the bar and linger there.

He watched the fair-haired man and his companions, who were now all seated at the table and ordering drinks from a scrawny waiter in a grubby apron. They looked darkly conspiratorial and were totally unaware that he was observing them. Lockhart searched his brain for the name mentioned by the pair at the campsite. It came – Dirksen!

So, the fair man with the bandage, his wife's killer, was Dirksen, and he was indeed keeping a rendezvous with assorted hard gentry here in dubious Salt Pass.

Lockhart shot another glance at the seated group. They were listening to Dirksen, who was talking earnestly. The whole tableau suggested a plot being laid.

All too aware that Dirksen might spot him in spite of his precautions, Lockhart knew he must get out of the saloon and gain time to plan his next move now that he had definitely located his wife's killer. He drained his glass and slipped away from the bar, keeping his back to the men at the table and moving behind groups of drinkers standing around.

He made a quick exit through the batwings and on to the gallery, now partially illumined by a slender crescent moon, and stopped short on almost colliding with a big man who was just stepping into the saloon.

The man gasped and drew back, startled. In the thin moonlight, Lockhart saw him become slack jawed in astonishment. He was the survivor of the pair who had tried to jump him at the campsite and whom Lockhart had left unconscious there. He was obviously about to join those keeping the rendezvous with Dirksen in the saloon.

He looked at Lockhart almost uncomprehendingly, giving him a split second in which to act.

Sapped of energy though he was after his recent hard travelling, he somehow found the speed and vigour to thump his fist into the man's belly with all his might.

The big man groaned and his body doubled forward as if hinged at the middle. Lockhart swung his fist at his jaw in an uppercut. For a second time, he floored the big saddle tramp, rendering him totally unconscious. The man slumped to the planking of the gallery like a felled tree.

The gallery and the portion of the street fronting it were empty and, collecting his wits, Lockhart was seized by the urgent need to get clear away before Dirksen and his companions in the saloon came out and discovered him, or before the man sprawled on the gallery recovered and alerted them to

Lockhart's presence in Salt Pass.

He quickly made for his hitched horse and saw, at the second hitch rack, two horses, one tied to the other by a rein and obviously a led animal – the mounts of the man he had just floored and that of his dead companion.

He wondered whether the saddle tramp had noticed his horse with its giveaway panniers, hitched at the other rack. Judging by the utter surprise on his face when they encountered each other, it seemed he had not. Possibly he was still too dulled by the blow from Lockhart's pistol back at the camp.

Mingled emotions roiled within Lockhart. There was his ever-present, aching impulse to avenge Marcy's killing by uncompromising and violent means; then there was the knowledge that, having at last tracked the killer, Dirksen, this far, he must somehow stick close to him and bide his time until he could strike at him.

Overriding those considerations, however, was the immediate need to distance himself from the saloon.

He made quickly for his hitched animal, released it, mounted and rode across the street which was still nearly empty. Directly across from the saloon there was a tall clapboard building, throwing a black shadow across an alley beside it. Lockhart headed his mount into the alley and halted it, well concealed by the shadows. From there he had a clear view of the entrance to the saloon, and he was reasonably sure that he could not be seen from that point.

He waited, holding down his impatience, his weariness and hunger with his gaze fixed on the frontage of the drinking den, hoping that Dirksen and his companions were not intent on a long night of drinking. After ten tense minutes, he was rewarded by the sight of them emerging on to the gallery, led by Dirksen.

'Hey, it's Lafe Fluter, out stone cold!' cried one in hoarse surprise.

Lockhart saw the figures on the shadowed gallery crowd around the unconscious man. He watched them haul him up to his feet and prop him against the rail of the gallery.

They busied themselves, shaking Fluter to revive him, all the time asking questions he could not answer. After several minutes he came round and his companions steadied him as he stumbled around uncertainly. Some of them stepped off the gallery and looked about the street, appparently seeking some sign of Fluter's attacker, but gave it up as a bad job. Five minutes later they mounted their animals, a couple helping Fluter to saddle up and cope with his led horse.

Dirksen's party swung their mounts about and faced the end of the street from which Lockhart had entered the town, spurred them into walking gait and, with Dirksen leading on his calico mare, headed off in the general direction of the Red River.

Lockhart waited until they rounded a bend and

were out of sight, then kneed his horse into a walk. He went steadily, determined to keep on Dirksen's track but aware that he must remain undetected. Round the bend, he saw them some distance ahead, they had not made for the ford giving access to Texas but were following an ill-defined trail running parallel to the river and between two hulking shoulders of land.

The trail eventually disappeared into moon-silvered rocks and thickly tangled brush.

He urged his weary animal onward, with the backs of Dirksen's party only just in view. He kept close to the shrubbery beside the trail which, this being fertile river bottomland, was fairly abundant and offered cover.

After ten minutes or so he saw the riders ahead disappear into another tangle of rocks and scrub at the base of the land bulking to the left of the trail, then Lockhart's horse quivered its lips in a whinny and a shiver ran through its whole frame. It sensed water and Lockhart saw that there was a small stream just visible in the rocks at the base of the slant of land to the right of the trail. The indications were that hard travelling had intensified his mount's thirst, so he halted, dismounted and led the animal to the stream, hoping that he would not wholly lose track of Dirksen's party.

He stood beside the animal, feeling utterly drained of energy.

Nevertheless, he was powered by his angry desire to keep on Dirksen's back and eventually gain a chance to wreak his revenge. He knew that was something he must cling to tenaciously in order to keep his determination from flagging and disintegrating.

At which point a heavy force hit the back of his neck in a savage rabbit-punch that sent him sprawling face first into the earth and the clumps of brush beside the stream.

His breath gusted out of him and he lay there, bewildered, with his senses swimming until he found the strength to roll over on to his back and look up.

Standing over him, with the thin moonlight touching glittering eyes and a high-cheekboned, impassive Indian face under a broad-brimmed hat, was a tall man, levelling a Henry rifle directly at his head.

CHAPTER FIVE

INTO THE HOLE

'Lie there still as a possum, mister,' said the man, keeping the Henry pointed dangerously close. 'Your panniers suggest you're a Texas Ranger but I don't see any badge and, anyway, Texas is over the river so you're off your jurisdiction. I want some answers. I watched you and that bunch of riders from up the slope there and I figured you were tailing them – or maybe you're one of them, straggling. All except Dirksen, leading them, are newcomers to The Hole, so maybe the whole bunch of you are reinforcements for the Colquitts. If you are a Ranger, tracking them all on your lonesome, you're a damn fool. Now give me some answers. What's going on at The Hole and who are you?'

A considerable amount of what the man said did not make sense to Lockhart, the more so because his brain was befuddled after the unexpected blow but he made a weak attempt to play for time.

'Who's asking?' he countered.

'Captain Jim Wing, United States Indian Police, that's who. Don't fool around with me. I want some answers. I take it as a personal insult that the Colquitt outfit established itself at The Hole, right here in the Choctaw Nation, and if they're building up their strength it makes things even worse. They've had too much of their own way already.'

Lockhart eased himself up to a sitting position. 'Dal Colquitt and his gang are finished, wiped out at Rock City by the Rangers and the citizens only few days ago,' he said.

The Indian policeman lowered his gun and his impassive expression changed to one of surprise. 'What? How do you know that?' he asked breathlessly.

'Got it from a Ranger captain named Thewlis, over at Squaw Creek. He was in on the fight.'

'So you *are* a Ranger! I know Thewlis, a good man, even if he is stiff-necked and not specially friendly to Indian folk. Like a lot of Texans, he can't forget that they had a long war with the Comanches. But the Colquitts wiped out – that's something new on me! I've been out this way on special assignment and had no contact with our headquarters for weeks. Probably even they don't know. You Rangers never hurry to tell us much unless it suits your purpose, but I reckon you know all about their mentality.' In spite of that comment, the Indian officer now appeared to be friendlier.

'I'm not a Ranger, even if those panniers are branding me as one. I just happen to have bought them cheap years ago.'

'Then who are you?'

'Dave Lockhart. I homesteaded at Blue Brush, Texas. The Colquitts raided and my wife was murdered by Dirksen who was riding with them. I was away from home and she tried to hold them off and hit Dirksen with a shot. The Colquitts went on to raid Rock City and rode into a trap. Thewlis said the Rangers were tipped off by an anonymous letter. Somehow, Dirksen survived and I've been trailing him ever since. I found he was meeting up with a bunch at the saloon in Salt Pass. Obviously, it was all prearranged.'

'Looks like you stuck to him like a fly on a honeypot,' said Wing, displaying some admiration. 'So Dirksen's showed up again on this side of the Red River, heading into The Hole with this new gang and you'd sure as hell put yourself in trouble if you followed him all the way into The Hole. You'd hardly get out of their hands alive.'

'Maybe I wasn't thinking any too straight. Having located Dirksen, I wasn't going to lose sight of him. I just want to avenge my wife, and I'll get him yet.'

'Damned if you haven't filled in some gaps in my knowledge, Mr Lockhart,' said the policeman. 'When did you last eat?'

'So long ago I almost can't remember.'

'I can remedy that,' said Jim Wing. 'Sorry I hit you but I'm glad to meet you.'

He extended a hand and helped Lockhart to stand, saying: 'Come with me. We have to make common cause and share what we know.'

He walked up the slope on to the dark tangles of brush, saplings and rocks with Lockhart following and leading his horse. In a small clearing, the fitful moon showed a rough brushwood shelter with a tethered horse beside it. A saddle and scattered equipment lay on the ground and when Lockhart glanced backwards and down, he saw that, from this position, an observer would have a view of the trail he had travelled and, on the further side of it, the tangle of rocks into which Dirksen and his party had disappeared.

This vantage point was so cunningly selected that anyone watching from it would be well covered even in broad daylight.

'I've been staked out here for days, watching comings and goings down at the entrance to The Hole and damn near been breathing down the necks of the bunch down there without their knowing it,' said Wing. 'It was Colquitt's crew until a few days ago. I guessed they'd taken off into Texas on a raiding spree but that Rock City tale is an eye-opener.'

Captain Jim Wing entered the shelter and gave his attention to lighting a small spirit stove, opening a can of beans and taking wrapped portions of food from a warsack. 'It'll be beans, pork, bread and coffee, nothing special but enough to fill you,' he stated as he worked. 'There's water and feed for your cayuse up here, too. Maybe it's not white man's luxury but I'm Choctaw and can live under a roof or under the stars. I use the spirit stove instead of a fire, so there's no smoke to give my position away and the camp is placed so the smell of my cooking doesn't drift toward The Hole.'

'I guess that's what's called an application of Indian savvy,' said Lockhart, 'but what is The Hole? I guess that's where Dirksen and his bunch have gone.'

'It's a network of tunnels and caves running right under the Red River,' answered Wing, tipping beans into a pan. 'One of the main entrances is right down there, hidden among the rocks where Dirksen's party went. There are several outlets on the other side of the river in Texas, all big enough for parties of riders to go through. One leads right into Smoke Canyon, which is mostly avoided by Texas folk because it's supposed to be haunted.'

'I heard tell of Smoke Canyon long ago,' Lockhart said. 'That was where a band of Comanches were massacred by the Texans and the US Army as I recall.'

'Sure, and the old ghost story helped to keep it good and isolated, which suited the Colquitt gang's purpose right down to the ground,' replied Wing.

Lockhart's head was clearer now and enlightenment was dawning. 'So while folk on the Texas side were puzzled about where the Colquitts crossed the river on their raids, they never figured they were not using a ford but going *under* the river?' he said.

Wing nodded and served up a couple of generous helpings of food with hunks of bread.

As they sat in the shelter eating, Wing said: 'It looks like Dirksen's taken over the Colquitts' operation and their headquarters, so I take it it's dawned on you who sent the Rangers that letter about the Rock City raid.'

'It could only be Dirksen,' Lockhart answered thoughtfully. 'He knew of the gang's plans and he must have blown the gaff on them even before they set off into Texas. Looks like he didn't do it for a reward, though.'

'No, you can bet he was out to take over Colquitt's entire operation,' said Jim Wing. 'A kind of legend has grown up that, wherever the Colquitt's hideout was, it'd be stuffed full of loot from raids not yet shared out and Dirksen knows it. I'll wager that he'll double deal this new gang and grab the whole lot when the time is ripe.'

'Yeah, Dirksen's obviously plenty brainy and treacherous,' agreed Lockhart.

He thought back over the sequence of time since he left Blue Brush and added: 'I had a brush with him at what must have been soon after the Rock City showdown, so he deserted the Colquitt gang between their raid on my place and the one on Rock City. He took a shot at me and vamoosed and now I reckon that was due to my panniers again. He probably saw them and thought the Rangers were scouting the country after the Rock City fight and

74

had caught up with him, they not knowing, of course, that he was their informer.'

Wing began pouring coffee. 'I'd say he had his double-dealing planned before the Colquitts went raiding,' he said. 'He must have made secret arrangements to gather his own gang in Salt Pass well beforehand. Treachery would come easy to Dirksen. I found he's known to the law elsewhere when I set out to investigate the Colquitts. First, he's not so young. He's a natural babyface, probably ten years older than he appears with plenty of villainous experience behind his youthful looks. Up Montana way he's called Kid Dirksen. He did prison time up there and, for sure, the gang he's collected here are old sidekicks from his criminal past. Looks like he built a network of them, then brought them into this country.'

'And they're probably every bit as bad as the Colquitts,' commented Lockhart.

'Maybe even worse if that's possible,' responded Wing. 'It galls me how easily that kind of gentry muscled in here, defiling the Choctaw Nation. We Choctaw knew about The Hole. It was an open tribal secret for years. At one time, the Comanches used it as a bolthole from the Texans. Some time back I figured the Colquitts had got in on the knowledge and were using The Hole, so I went off on my private assignment and I found I was right.'

'How come your force never rounded them up?' asked Lockhart.

Jim Wing gave a sardonic laugh. 'That's due to

75

various complications because Indian Territory law's a damned mess. Federal law here and in Oklahoma Territory is administered by Judge Isaac Parker, far away in Fort Smith, Arkansas, and the judge's marshals are thin on the ground. Then there's our outfit, the US Indian Police. We started out as tribal forces called Light Horse bands, only active each within its own tribal nation. We got a bit more strength with federal backing but we're too few and badly equipped.'

Wing waved his knife in angry gesture. 'Would you believe, I can't even get my section of the outfit equipped with a telegraph? We're deeply entangled in political complications and jealousies about various jurisdictions. A man working alone hits problems aplenty. I couldn't even muster enough officers to make a decisive raid on the Colquitts though I located their headquarters. I've been watching and waiting for my chance to act and now I find the game has changed with the Colquitts gone and a new set of robbers spoiling for trouble. And I knew nothing about it until you showed up. Well, by thunder, I'll settle the account of Dirksen's bunch before they get even halfway as powerful as Dal Colquitt's crew.'

'You've got an ally,' stated Lockhart with grim-faced firmness.

'I need one,' said Jim Wing. 'I know you have a plenty big grudge and it's plain that you can stick to your purpose. It'll mostly be just you and me against the whole gang. How are your tracking skills?'

'I soldiered against the Apaches in Arizona Territory and learned a few things.'

'Don't tell me you bluebellies out-tracked the Apaches because I won't believe you.'

'We didn't. They outsmarted us often enough to teach us lessons in keeping out of sight, being patient, missing nothing and moving fast when the time was absolutely right.'

Wing nodded approvingly. 'Good. Keep it all in mind. We sleep tonight and tomorrow we set about getting our teeth into Kid Dirksen and his ugly friends.'

They spread their bedrolls under the brush shelter. After the exertions of the day, Lockhart slept soundly, awakening to find Jim Wing already active and the smell of coffee and bacon in the air.

In bright sunlight Wing was busy at the portable stove. 'Get your handgun loaded and if you need extra shells, I have a supply,' he said. 'We're going into The Hole for a look-see.'

'Into The Hole?' echoed Lockhart.

'Sure. There are several ways in. I know them all. I grew up here and went in and out as a kid, well before the place became an outlaw hang-out. See that ridge on the opposite side of the trail, right above where you saw Dirksen's gang disappear? There are several ways in from up there. We Choctaw know them all but the guys in there will know nothing about them. There's something else. In the night, I heard horses on the trail below, sneaked a look and saw three riders heading for the

77

entrance down there. Must be late recruits for Dirksen who'd told them how to reach The Hole.'

'Three new arrivals,' mused Lockhart. 'That'll make eight in all, including Dirksen.'

After a quick breakfast they made their way cautiously down the slope to the trail.

Then they moved swiftly up the opposite slope to its scrub-covered crest immediately above the point where Dirksen's bunch rose into the concealed entrance to The Hole. Jim Wing stopped at a large, flat, circular stone and gestured to his companion to help him lift it. They hauled it upwards and Lockhart saw that it formed a kind of manhole cover, protecting a round, well-like shaft dropping through dry, root-cluttered soil.

'A way in,' said Wing. 'Generations of Choctaw have known about it. Climb down there and move silently, Apache fashion. I'll follow you.'

Lockhart scrambled down the opening, through earth and straggling roots and dropped into a small and gloomy cave-like chamber where he could breathe easily. Wing came down after him in a lithe, silent fashion.

'Keep your voice down,' whispered Wing, 'and move slowly.'

Lockhart's eyes adjusted to the gloom and he looked around. This chamber had an opening at one end through which could be seen the rock wall of what was obviously a far larger cavern. Thin scarlet-and-yellow light flickered on its walls, as if from a fire somewhere down below in the bigger chamber. Echoing up from the depths outside the cave were strong voices in loud discussion, suggesting a number of men engaged in an argument.

'This is one of the smaller caves in the place,' whispered Jim Wing. 'The main chamber is below us. It's a natural campsite. There's water trickling in from the river. Horses can drink it and so can humans if it's boiled. As I thought, they're using it as their hang-out, simply taking over the Colquitt gang's set-up.'

He waved towards the jagged opening at the further end of the cave. 'There's a ledge outside this place. From it, you can look down and see what's going on below. Crawl on your belly out to the ledge and take a look but go carefully. Take your hat off and watch out that the firelight down there doesn't show you up.'

The pair, hatless to reduce the chances of their being seen from below, moved to the opening of the cave, dropped to their stomachs and inched their way outside. They were on an elevated ledge on a rock wall of a cavern as big as a cathedral and deep in shadow, though the opposite wall of the cavern was illuminated by the flames of a large campfire below.

The firelight showed tethered horses, weapons, and boxes of supplies stacked against one wall. There were bedrolls spread around. The aroma of recently cooked food drifted upwards and eight men squatted or stood around the fire. Lockhart recognized Dirksen, limned by the flames, standing in a commanding position

'You were right, there's eight in all,' whispered Jim Wing.

The men's voices were carried up, amplified within the rugged walls and one rose forcefully above the rest. Lockhart saw that it was Dirksen who was holding forth. He had shed his bandage now and the uncertain light of the fire showed an ugly weal at his temple.

'. . . no, I say the Ace High mine is the best bet. It's in isolated country and easy to hit,' Dirksen was saying. 'There's every chance of a payroll and, if there isn't, there's bound to be money in the offices.'

'No, Kid,' came a firm objection from a big man squatting close to the fire.

Lockhart recognized him as Fluter, the man he had knocked unconscious at his overnight damp and again on the gallery of the Salt Pass saloon.

'That's all too much of a maybe,' continued Fluter. 'Squaw Crossing is the place to hit, right after the trail herd has gone through. Me and Charlie saw cowpokes spending in the saloons; trail bosses buying up gear at the last minute and money flowing every whichway – you know how trail towns are when a drive goes through. There's only one bank in the place and the merchants will have stuffed it fatter than a Thanksgiving turkey. Charlie'd tell you, except that damned guy killed him. The town has an old-timer of a marshal and a couple of deputies. If we plan it right, we can bust that bank easy! Me and Charlie never saw a better bank more ready to be cracked—'

'Oh, sure. You and Charlie specialized in banks, didn't you, Fluter?' cut in Dirksen with a hint of sarcasm. 'But the pair of you still drew a stretch in the pokey, where I met you.'

'Not for a bank job, Kid,' objected big Fluter indignantly. 'We stepped outside our field, trying a stage hold-up. We did seven banks before that and got clean away every time.'

'Fluter could be right, Kid,' said another of the crew. 'The Ace High mine might look easy but we don't know for sure that there's any *dinero* there. That Squaw Crossing bank sounds a sure-fire prospect.'

'Sure,' piped up another. 'And one ancient town marshal with a couple of deputies don't sound like much opposition against eight of us acting fast and to a plan. With the town slack and dozy after the trail herd has gone through, this could be our chance.'

Kid Dirksen stood in thought for a moment. 'Yeah, it's tempting but just suppose we hit the town when it ain't slack and dozy. Suppose we ride in just when there's another trail herd on the move and the place is stuffed with armed cowpokes.'

'There's no herd due to cross the Red until another week,' declared Fluter. 'Me and Charlie made enquiries out of force of habit when we saw that bank. It's on a corner of the main drag, easy to get at and easy to get away from. The town'll be sleepy and just plain begging on its knees to be hit.'

'A ride to Squaw Crossing from here will mean a night camp,' protested another man.

'If we push the pace over the back trails, we can do it with only a couple of hours' rest,' said Dirksen, obviously warming to the notion of a raid on Squaw Crossing. He paused, then affirmed his conversion to the idea by saying: 'Yeah, let's go for that bank in Squaw Crossing and bust it! Hell, we're younger and smarter than Dal Colquitt's bunch. They were mostly a set of old-timers who somehow managed to dodge slugs and the hangman for too long.'

'The suckers don't know how he fixed the odds against the Colquitts,' whispered Wing, lying flat alongside Lockhart. 'And he'll double-cross this bunch in his own good time.'

From their shadow-enshrouded perch near the roof of the cavern, Lockhart and Wing listened to the echoing voices drifting upwards. Lockhart's trigger-finger itched. He knew that from this ledge he could shoot the standing Dirksen easily, but he kept a tight grip on his seething lust for vengeance and followed the echoing verbal exchanges.

'So he's fallen for the Squaw Crossing move,' murmured Wing into his ear.

Now Lockhart felt intense anxiety for the town for Marshal Bill Ritter and particularly for Helen. Time and again since he left Squaw Crossing Helen had come unbidden into his mind.

'I guess we can plot their next move easily

enough,' whispered Wing. 'Away behind them are several natural tunnels, all going under the river to the Texas side. One leads into Smoke Canyon, one to the edge of the Staked Plains and the others to various back trails. I figure they'll see the Smoke Canyon one as the most convenient.'

They watched Dirksen, pondering in silence briefly, then he said decisively: 'OK, Squaw Crossing will be our first big job and it looks like a chance for a good haul. We move off around noon, travel fast, make night camp for a couple of hours, then hit the town just as the stores and the bank open. We plan the hit, knowing just who goes into the bank and who guards the street – and we make sure we take care of that old lawman and his deputies as soon as they show their noses. Every man will have a job and every man will do his job.'

The firelight touched Kid Dirksen's deceptively youthful face as he struck an arrogant pose before his newly gathered bunch of armed henchmen. 'Sure thing,' he crowed. 'That little old town will be dozing after fattening its bank on the passing beef on the hoof; dozing like a hog after a feed. Well, we'll sure awaken it. Squaw Crossing's bank is going to know that the Dirksen crew is opening its business account!'

Suddenly, Lockwood had a vision of his wife, gasping her last breath in his arms and an agonized rush of emotions surged through his brain. He had trailed Marcy's killer for many arduous and danger-fraught miles with only the remotest hope of discovering him.

Now, fate had put her killer within pistol range of him, swaggering and boasting of perpetrating robbery and mayhem against a town that had showed itself to be friendly towards Lockhart, and where two people in particular, the courageous and enigmatic Helen Ritter and her veteran lawman father had earned his gratitude and loyalty.

Though he tried to keep it in check, his temper swelled, becoming like an overburdened dam about to burst. Suddenly, he had the urge to shoot Dirksen now that he had him virtually at his mercy, highlighted by the flames of the fire and impossible to miss from this elevated position. He screwed his eyes to take measure of Dirksen as a target for a pistol shot.

His hand twitched down towards his holstered Colt but Wing, sprawled beside him, saw the movement and made a grab for his arm. He clutched it and held it firmly.

'No!' he whispered urgently. 'Not here!'

'Hell, why not?' hissed Lockhart. 'We could pick off the whole bunch of them before they even knew we'd opened fire.'

'Sure we could – and we'd likely bring the whole damn cave down on us. This whole system of caverns is as rotten as a mouldy cheese,' Wing pointed out. 'Take my word for it; the Choctaw people have known them for years. Start any gunplay in here and there'll surely be reverberations causing falls of rock that'll either kill

84

us or entomb us alive.'

Growling his discontent, Lockhart stilled his hand.

'Patience,' counselled Jim Wing. 'Now we know what they plan to do, we can scoot out of here. Slither back the way we came in.'

Both men inched back into the small cave on their bellies. Standing as best they could in the cramped space, Lockhart was boosted by Wing into the well-like shaft and emerged into the sunlight. With lithe ease, Wing came up the outlet after him.

Lockhart felt resentment at being deprived of his attempt to shoot Dirksen, yet it was mixed with appreciation of Wing's superior knowledge of what was, after all, his natural ground. Furthermore, he had to admit that his lust for vengeance would not be fully satisfied by killing Dirksen with a sudden shot out of the darkness of the cavern. Ideally, when he settled his score with the baby-faced killer, he wanted to face him and let him know why he was being paid in the brutal coinage he fully deserved.

He beat soil and sand from himself and faced Jim Wing with some slight hostility though a more reasoning part of him acknowledged that the policeman had a firm grip on what he was about. The US Indian Police might not stand high in the estimation of other Western law-enforcement bodies but Wing's patient and painstaking following of the Colquitt gang to the extent of researching the criminal past of its members showed an approach to police work lacking elsewhere.

There was no doubt that, given time and resources enough to put the gang before a court, he would have achieved a string of hangings. As it was, they had perished in swift, bullet-bitten action, prompted by an anonymous letter from one of their own treacherous kind.

Jim Wing was a lawman of ability and Lockhart was coming to value his professionalism and his companionship and his Indian know-how in this dangerous environment.

'Well?' asked Lockhart. 'Dirksen's bunch aims to attack Squaw Crossing tomorrow morning. How do we stop them? We're outnumbered and on the wrong side of the Red River.'

'The odds are against us for sure,' agreed Wing. 'We're only on the fringe of the Choctaw nation here and far from the nearest tribal township. There's no chance of raising a Choctaw posse. Salt Pass is totally lawless. It was just a grubby settlement beside the ford until the Civil War. Then deserters from both sides and other renegades took it over. It's been no good ever since. It'll never produce a posse. No, it's the two of us against the Dirksen gang, so we have to act fast to get to Squaw Crossing before tomorrow's sunup, alert the town and arrange a welcome with hot lead when they arrive.'

Lockhart stared at him. Wing seemed to be making scant sense. Dirksen and his gang were doubtless already making ready to depart from The Hole by the outlets to the Texas side of the river and embark on a long ride entailing an overnight camp, yet Wing was talking of being on the scene when they arrived at Squaw Crossing.

'How do we do that?' he asked with incredulity written all over his face.

Captain Jim Wing's face broke its impassive Indian mould to display the ghost of a smile. 'First, we collect our horses, gather some grub and ammunition, then we take the river route,' he replied enigmatically.

CHAPTER SIX

THE RIVER ROUTE

On the Indian Territory side of the Red River, beside a snaking trail, a small cabin stood in the shade of a stand of live oaks. Behind the structure was a pier made of planks to which a flatboat was moored. It was like all river flatboats, by no means a sleek craft. A crude, raftlike construction of logs with a slant-roofed deckhouse situated at its stem near its cumbersome hand-operated rudder arrangement, it was typical of the heavy-duty vessels of pioneer origin that carried people and cargoes along the countless miles of Western American rivers.

Today, the flatboat rode easily and lazily on the rise and fall of the river's current.

Taking his ease on a stool outside the door of the cabin was an old pipe-smoking Choctaw Indian. He wore a high-crowned hat from under which beaded braids of white hair hung down to each shoulder. His outfit was broadly that of a white Westerner except for a buckskin vest embellished with beads and river shells. His lean face with its high cheekbones was seamed by deep wrinkles and weathered by decades of suns and storms.

There was no telling the age of Old Sam Crowfeather and he never disclosed it. Some said that, in his tender years, he had even walked the bitter 'Trail of Tears' when the evicted tribes were forcibly transplanted from their rich Southern lands that they had held from time immemorial to the empty Indian Territory.

Aged though he was, Old Sam had a tough and resilient body and an intellect in no way dimmed by the passing of time. His serene face showed the wisdom of years.

Seated outside his cabin, Old Sam appeared to be half-dozing as he smoked, but his ears were attuned to the natural sounds around him and his eyes flickered open when he heard the mounting drumming of approaching horses. The sound indicated two riders.

The old man watched a far bend in the trail and saw a pair of horsemen raising the dust at a smart clip. One was in nondescript black clothing with no badges visible, but Old Sam recognized him as Captain Jim Wing.

The second might have been a homesteader or a cowhand but the panniers slapping the side of his mount suggested a Texas Ranger, though, again, he displayed no badge. Both horsemen bore bedrolls and saddle gear betokening relatively lengthy travelling ahead of them.

The riders pulled rein outside the cabin and the dark-clad one raised a hand in greeting.

'Howdy, Cap'n Wing,' called Old Sam. 'You ain't been this way in a long time. Is your friend a Ranger? We don't often have Rangers on this side of the Red. Must be something big afoot.'

'Howdy, Old Sam. Yes, there's something afoot. This here's Dave Lockhart. He's a Texas man but no Ranger,' said Wing. 'Is that floating woodpile of yours in working order? We need to go down river and fast.'

'Sure, she's in order and she's no woodpile. She's as elegant afloat as any three-masted masted schooner,' declared Old Sam. He raised his voice and bellowed lustily: 'Dan, come on out and meet some company. Before you do, put a light under that pot of stew and get ready to serve a couple of doses of it with bread and coffee.'

From the cabin there emerged a strapping, broad-shouldered Choctaw, probably in his thirties, who nodded a greeting to Wing and Lockhart.

'You know my grandson, Cap'n Jim. He does the heavy work aboard the vessel. What's this trip you have to make?'

'We have to be in Squaw Crossing before sunup tomorrow.'

'Can't be done,' responded Old Sam firmly. 'The river's running strong enough but last winter's big

90

storms blew a bunch of trees into the stream. They're still there, causing a total blockage at Boulder Bend. I reckon even the fish have a hard time getting past it. Dan and me can get you as far as Boulder Bend and no further. From there, you'll have to ride to Squaw Crossing. Riding flat out along the river bottomlands will get you there quickest.'

'That's a tolerable hard ride but I guess we have no choice. We're in a hell of a hurry,' commented Wing.

'Then feed and water your horses. A full belly can keep a cayuse from getting too nervous on a long river voyage,' Old Sam said. 'Setting off around now, we can get to Boulder Bend about the fall of night, but eat first of all.'

Inside the cabin, Lockhart and Wing, seated at a rough wooden table, were given full bowls of stew with bread and coffee by the hulking, muscular and mostly silent Dan Crowfeather. Sitting across from them, Old Sam said weightily: 'Something you maybe ought to know, Cap'n Jim, is that there's been talk along the river of the Bexley clan showing up again. Talk is they've been lurking around the river bottoms. Seems they've been off somewhere, New Mexico maybe, doing something or other. Something lawless, I don't doubt.'

Jim Wing paused in his eating and said: 'The Bexleys, eh? Well that's right interesting, Old Sam. Thanks for the information.' His face remained impassive but Lockhart noted the deep thoughtfulness in the slowness of his delivery. 'They're no-account and their crimes are penny-ante stuff.'

'Sure, Seth was the really dangerous one and he's no more. But the rest are pretty damned poisonous and they sure as hell don't like you, Cap'n,' said Old Sam.

'And they have mighty good cause not to,' Wing replied wryly.

Twenty minutes later the four walked the horses aboard the flatboat, secured them to the pole rail that ran around the craft and relieved them of their saddles and trail-gear.

Old Sam stationed himself at the swinging bar controlling the rudder and, using a stout peeled pole that looked long enough to touch the bottom of the deep river, Dan shoved the whole craft away from the pier and into the swiftly flowing stream. Flatboat, passengers and cargo began to float southward with Old Sam deftly controlling the rudder to keep the craft in the strongest run of the current.

As the two experienced Indians set about navigating the flatboat, Lockhart asked Wing, dubiously: 'D'you figure we can get to Squaw Crossing before Dirksen's bunch hit the town?'

'Just about. They're sure to take the trail you rode – the one that took you to the ford at Salt Pass. It's above us in the higher ground and it's long and twisted. The river runs straighter and, with this fast current running, we should go faster than any riders, but the blockage means we can't get past Boulder Bend. We'll have to press our horses mighty hard on a ride through the bottomlands in the night but that suits me. Being white men, Dirksen's bunch will naturally choose the trail on the higher ground. White men travel thinking of good campsites and waterholes. An Indian would choose to travel over the bottomlands. It's harder but more direct than the trail.'

The sun rose to its zenith as the flatboat rode on the swift current. Lockhart and Wing occasionally helped out the mostly silent Dan in the task of shoving the craft clear of large rocks that humped out of the stream, each using one of the lengthy poles.

At the stern, Old Sam laboured with an energy belied by his aged frame, swinging the cumbersome tiller bar with a skill born of years of river navigation and Lockhart watched the two Indians work with a natural ease. He realized that their skill sprang from an uncanny knowledge of the river or, perhaps, an inbuilt affinity with it.

This relationship with the river seemed akin to an Indian's affinity with the landscape as a whole. Something innate in them engendered a sympathy with the very spirit of the long, swirling and age-old watercourse. They and it shared a oneness that allowed them to ride its moods and dangers without fear and almost as a part of it.

Now and then Jim Wing glanced at the sky, seeming to calculate the passage of time as if he, too, had some inborn ethnic ability and the lush river bottomlands slid past rapidly.

Much of the time Wing sat in the shade of the deckhouse, silent and seeming to look blankly into space. He was practising the same apparent withdrawal from the here and now that Lockhart had seen among the desert tribes of the South-west, a form of something like meditation peculiar to the Indians.

Lockhart wished he knew the secret of it, since it seemed to put a man at a distance from whatever might be an immediate trouble and to rest his anxieties. It reminded him that Wing might be a policeman who showed that he had sharp and practical approaches to policing, like his desire for more modem resources for the Indian Police and his researching of men he tracked, but he was also an Indian. He was in tune with the landscape he existed in and was almost a part of it.

The sun lowered and was sinking and Wing was alert when the flatboat reached a wide bend. Rearing out of the water ahead was an intimidating barrier of tree trunks and branches, totally blocking the passage of the craft.

'There they are, the trees blown in by the storms,' said Old Sam. 'We can't get past them and they'll snarl us if we run into 'em. Shove into the shore quick, Dan.'

Dan Crowfeather, Wing and Lockhart wielded their cumbersome poles, reaching the bed of the river and forcing the flatboat towards the Texas shore. Dusk was deepening as the craft touched ground and Wing and Lockhart unhitched their horses and led them ashore. From inside his vest Wing took a booklet and a pencil and began to write, then he tore off the page and handed it to Old Sam.

'This'll get you payment for the trip and for feed for the horses from Indian Police headquarters,' he said.

The old Indian nodded. 'Sure. I know the police will pay. I trust 'em, though I know there's those on this side of the river who don't like you stepping into the territory of the Rangers. Watch out, Cap'n Wing, whatever antic you're planning.'

'We will,' replied Wing. 'You and Dan take care how you go back upriver against those currents during the night.'

'We know how to do it after all our time on the river,' rumbled Old Sam as he and his grandson shoved off from the bank to work the flatboat's return to their base.

Lockhart and Wing secured their saddles and trappings on the horses again and lost no time in mounting up and riding off through thickening gloom, riding over the loamy soil of the river shore, heading south.

Lockhart felt an acute apprehension at being back on the soil of Texas.

He had made his home in this state but he had also killed a man here not too many hours before. The circumstances were such that he might claim self-defence but there were no witnesses so he might equally feel the full weight of Texas law. He still remembered the warning of Ranger Captain Fred Thewlis concerning a Texas hangrope.

The river was to their left and there were heavy growths of trees and shrubbery on their right. They rode in silence with their animals, rested by the trip along the river.

They were making good time when Wing suddenly drew rein and gestured to Lockhart to do the same.

Wing sat still, listening then he whispered: 'There are horses ahead.'

Lockhart could hear nothing. 'How do you know?' he asked, imitating Wing's low whisper.

'You sure didn't pick up much Indian savvy from those Apaches if you didn't notice our horses quivering their lips and pricking their ears?' said Wing. 'They're aware of other horses in the vicinity. And I've been seeing signs of this land being recently travelled for some time. Not just hoofprints. Someone's recently been spitting tobacco juice on the ground. Slacken speed and look out for trouble.'

Significantly, Wing nudged his Colt loose in its holster, prompting Lockhart to do the same.

They continued on at a slower pace, then they heard the sound of approaching riders. The unmistakable tramping of horses and jingling of ringbits heralded the approach of a party of five horsemen, who appeared out of the gloom. Their leader was a big man who stood in his stirrups, bent his body forward as if to better scrutinize the approaching pair, then, with a grating cackle of laughter, called: 'Well, look at who we have riding up close to us!' He waved his arm, causing his companions to fan out and ride abreast, making a tight barrier across the trail.

In the fast-failing light the riders looked a wholly unsavoury crew.

They were clad in nondescript range garb, decked out with a variety of weaponry and their unshaven faces under the wide brims of their sombreros were stamped by what was obviously a family likeness.

As they approached, line abreast, Lockhart saw that the big man, now in the middle of the line, was flanked by a pair nearer his own age, but two much younger men were positioned one at either end of the line.

The riders continued to approach Lockhart and Wing, strung across the trail, then they hauled their reins, halting their animals and totally blocking the way of the advancing pair. Lockhart and Wing rode on to face them.

Wing hissed: 'I knew it. It's the Bexleys. Keep your wits about you, there's bad blood between this bunch and me. The one in the middle is the eldest brother, Bud. He'll make big talk, but he's dangerous. The two on either side of him are his brothers, Skeeter and Horace, both pure poison.'

Wing paused, quickly considered the whole party,

then hissed: 'The two younger ones at the end are new to me. I don't know whether they're dangerous or not. They look like cousins and the Bexleys operate as a clan. If you ever made a quick draw get ready to make one before we get out of this. They would skin me alive if they could. Watch Skeeter and Horace. They might try to pull something while Bud talks, as he's sure to. And keep an eye on the younger pair.'

Wing pulled rein only yards in front of the line of Bexleys and Lockhart followed suit. Wing called boldly: 'Get out of the way. You're blocking our path!'

'We aim to,' hooted Bud Bexley with a grating cackle of laughter.

Then he pronounced slowly and chillingly: 'We just can't believe our luck, having Sergeant Jim Wing of the Injun so-called Police delivered into our hands.'

'It's Captain Wing, now, you'll be pleased to know, Bud,' corrected Wing. 'Move your horses – pronto!'

'*Captain* Wing,' echoed Bud Bexley. 'I suppose they promoted you for leaving your mud pile across the river and hanging good white men. So now you're in Texas again, with a fellow tricked out with Rangers' panniers but he's no Ranger because I don't see a badge and no Ranger rides without his badge. Why're you on this side of the Red where Injuns are not wanted?' He paused and spat on the ground.

'Injuns!' he snorted. 'We had enough of you Injuns from the Nations when your Comanche friends were killing Texan women and kids.'

He spat again, putting eloquent and vindictive meaning into the act. 'You sheltered them damned Comanches after they scooted over the river,' he accused.

'The Comanches were not our friends,' replied Wing. 'Sure, they holed up with us, uninvited, and we advised them to give up their old raiding ways and take to our ways – to settle in towns and take up farming. But you know all that and I'm not about to discuss Indian affairs with you. You're just a windbag, Bud. I know there's a matter you really want to get down to. So, if you're hankering to do business on that score, let's get to it. Otherwise, you and your kin move your horses and let us pass.'

Bud Bexley leered. 'You're damned right we have business with you, Wing – the business of settling with you for the way you hanged our brother, Seth.'

'I didn't hang Seth. You know damned well he was hanged by your own Texas law and quite properly. He murdered a harmless Choctaw man here in Texas. I tracked him down and handed him to Texas lawmen, all proper and legal,' stated Jim Wing, showing flat-out defiance of Bud Bexley's belligerence.

Dave Lockhart felt an icy trickle down his spine as he saw Wing's right hand inching towards the Colt at his belt as he spoke. Apparently deliberately pushing for trouble, Wing repeated: 'So, either get down to business or get out of our path.'

Bud Bexley drew back his lips in a snarl of hatred. Then he made a swift grab at his holster.

CHAPTER SEVEN

GUNSMOKE INTERLUDE

Jim Wing's hand was quicker. It dived, then came up, filled with a barking Colt that split the gathering dusk with a vivid lance of muzzle-fire.

Bud Bexley, with his mouth wide open and his eyes already dead, lurched back in his saddle as his horse pranced back on its hind legs in the face of the close-range shot.

For an instant, Lockhart seemed to be reliving elements of his time amid the powdersmoke and bullets of the campaign against the Apaches. Almost before he knew it, he was crouching low in his saddle and hauling his six-gun from leather as, through a scarf of gunsmoke, he glimpsed Horace Bexley flourishing his pistol and aiming it at Wing.

The policeman was in the act of discharging a

second shot that sent Skeeter Bexley lurching to one side, then slithering out of his saddle. Lockhart fired instinctively and heard Horace Bexley give an agonized croak as he threw his six-gun in the air and fell dead over his saddle horn.

In swirling gunsmoke and the blasting of weapons, the horses of all the riders jerked and kicked. Fighting to control his animal, Lockhart heard a drumming of hoofs. He caught a brief glimpse of the two younger members of the Bexley crew, white-faced with fear, plunging their animals in panicky retreat into the shadowy trees at one side of the trail.

'Let 'em go,' growled Wing. 'They're wet-behind-the-ears kids and scared as jackrabbits, though I suppose, in a few years, they'll be as obnoxious as the rest of the Bexley clan.'

The bullet-punctured mêlée was so swift and over so quickly as almost to bewilder Lockhart. He could scarcely believe the manner in which he had been involved in it, thrust into almost unthinking action by Jim Wing's prodding of the Bexley faction.

He controlled his spooked horse and called to Wing, almost accusingly: 'You pushed it! You got me tangled up in that ruckus before I knew it by the way you goaded Bud Bexley.'

Wing calmed his own horse and stated: 'Sure I did. For the last couple of years the Bexleys have been swearing they'll get me for the way I arrested Seth because he killed a harmless old Choctaw man here in Texas and Texas law dragged its feet over it.

102

None of 'em ever had the guts to cross the river into the Nations to look for me. When I saw the whole crew, with a couple of relatives for added weight, I just knew they'd get to smoking it out because they thought the odds were all on their side and they couldn't lose. I figured there was no point in delaying the showdown.'

'I'm no gunfighter,' objected Lockhart. 'How did you know I'd be of any use in backing your play in a corner as tight as that one?'

Wing gave him his expressionless Indian stare.

'It was just plain logic. I know your calibre and was plumb sure you'd rise to the occasion,' he responded matter-of-factly. 'Any man who soldiered through the Apache campaign and survived it must have acquired gun savvy worth taking a chance on.'

Before Lockhart had time to bask in Wing's apparent high opinion of him, the policeman came down from his saddle quickly and gave his attention to the situation as it stood after the fight with the Bexleys. Two restless horses, those of Bud and Horace Bexley, each with a body humped in its saddle, were pawing at the earth and a third, that of Skeeter Bexley, stood riderless, its owner sprawling dead on the ground.

Lockhart climbed down from his mount and surveyed this aftermath of the violent action. 'What do we do? Bury them?' he asked.

'No time for that,' said Wing. 'Lay them beside the trail. Take the saddles and gear off the horses and stash them with the bodies, then leave the horses to graze. Maybe those Bexley kids will eventually find the guts to creep back here and they can take care of things. We have to get to Squaw Crossing, remember?'

It came to Lockhart that, for a second time, he had perpetrated a killing here in Texas and his conscience was disturbed. Paradoxically, he had to admit that he fully planned to shoot Marcy's murderer without compunction, but his path to vengeance had taken strange and bloody turns, making him more of a killer than he ever intended to be. And Kid Dirksen was still on the loose.

'This'll sure put us in bad with the law here in Texas,' he ventured.

Captain Jim Wing gave a sharp laugh. 'It was plain self-defence. The whole bunch of 'em wanted trouble from the start and Bud Bexley went to draw first. Texas lawmen won't be too worried by the dispatch of the Bexleys and they'll even take the word of an Indian policeman on what happened here. Time is wasting. C'mon, let's get to it, then light out for Squaw Crossing, fast as we can.'

On the winding trail above the Red River bottomlands a short time before Lockhart and Wing clashed with the Bexleys, a couple of riders made their way through the falling shades of night. One was the hulking Lafe Fluter, who had twice suffered the indignity of being knocked senseless by Dave Lockhart. His companion was Shorty Diggs, an old and villainous prison associate of Kid Dirksen, now recruited to the gang he had formed.

The two had been detailed by Dirksen to go ahead of the main party and scout out a suitable spot for their night camp. Fluter was chosen because he had some prior knowledge of the trail. Diggs was sent more or less to approve his choice since Fluter was weak on brains save for a remarkable skill at planning bank robberies, which was why Dirksen selected him when plotting his takeover of Dal Colquitt's operations.

Fluter experienced severe misgivings on this trail. He felt it might well be haunted. Somewhere close to this spot the plans of his sidekick, Charlie Clashman, and himself had gone badly wrong when they attempted to jump the lone traveller with the horse panniers.

Charlie had wound up dead and the stranger had all but brained Fluter with a pistol.

When he came to, Fluter solved the problem of Charlie's body by hauling it down to the river and sinking it, having weighted it with heavy stones to prevent its eventually surfacing near one of the settlements downriver. Fluter was superstitious and not at all happy about riding a trail that held such dark and ominous memories. If Charlie's spectre haunted this locality, it might not be at all pleased with Fluter's unceremonious handling of the mortal remains of his long-time partner in crime.

He and Diggs had left the rest of Dirksen's party some distance behind when they heard the unmistakable cracking of six-guns from some way ahead.

'Something's going on up yonder,' muttered Diggs, alarmed.

'Better go easy. Might be the law,' cautioned Fluter. Both riders slackened the pace of their horses.

They rode on at a slow walk, listening to a further couple of bursts of gunfire. Then there was silence. They covered a mile or so, travelling cautiously and hearing no more distant shooting.

'Seems to be all over,' said Diggs and, heartened, they carried on riding more boldly. Quite suddenly they rounded a bend in the trail and in the gloom discerned two young men, unmounted and allowing their lathered and sweating horses to catch their breaths. They had a variety of arms and, so far as could be judged in the poor light, their whole appearance suggested young owlhooters.

Neither Fluter nor Diggs liked young outlaws. They were prone to recklessness, always had ideas above their station and could lead old and cautious criminals into trouble. It was pretty clear to Diggs and Fluter that this pair had some connection with the shooting they'd heard only recently. The two Dirksen men rode towards the younger pair with some caution.

There was equal caution on the side of the brothers Will and Joe Tooley, cousins of the Bexleys out of New Mexico. Both were in their early twenties and had but lately started riding with their cousins, who were flamboyant but low-level desperadoes.

With the exception of the murder committed by the late Seth Bexley, the whole Bexley clan had never distinguished itself in the dubious annals of crime and most of their shabby exploits were perpetrated outside their native Texas, over the border in the desert settlements of New Mexico, well out of reach of the Texas Rangers.

Now Will and Joe were thoroughly scared after seeing their older cousins so speedily dispatched by the pair of riders who had come out of the gloom. They scooted out of the Red River bottoms, forcing their horses up through the shrubbery and trees to the trail on the higher ground. They knew that, somewhere up there, a trail eventually leading back to New Mexico branched off and they were out to find it.

Stopping on the broader trail to blow their horses, they were overtaken by clan loyalty and were debating the very point Wing had mentioned.

They figured they ought to return to the scene of the battle with the strangers and bury the bodies of their kinsmen as decently as they could.

The shooting had stopped and the strangers had probably left the scene by this time. The brothers were considering whether or not it was safe to return. And now, disconcertingly, another pair of strangers had emerged from the gathering gloom.

'Who're you fellers ?' called Lafe Fluter from his saddle.

'Just a couple of travelling guys,' replied Will Tooley. He was wary of this pair and resolved to give nothing away.

'We heard shooting,' called Shorty Diggs. 'Know anything about it?'

Joe Tooley, still badly scared and not so keenly intelligent as his brother, blurted out: 'We were travelling with our kin and two fellers jumped us back yonder and killed our three cousins—'

'What kind of fellers were they?' cut in Fluter.

'It seems one was a kind of policeman and the other had horse panniers like Rangers have—' gabbled Joe until his brother nudged his arm to shut him up.

'Panniers?' queried Fluter. The word revived memories of the attempt by Charlie Clashman and himself to jump the lone traveller making camp beside this very trail, the very man whom he had glimpsed just before he was knocked cold a second time on the gallery of the saloon in Salt Pass. If this locality was not haunted by Charlie Clashman, he thought, it seemed to be haunted by that damned man with the panniers.

'Jumped by a couple of hardcases,' said Shorty Diggs. 'Just goes to show how you never know what ruffians might be riding around these parts.' This was delivered with a mock gravity that Diggs thought was funny.

Fluter was less amused. The mysterious man with the panniers was beginning to assume the proportions of his nemesis. Twice Fluter had encountered him and twice he had suffered and now there was news of him in this vicinity with

someone disturbingly described as a policeman.
This pair might be met up with further along the
trail. If there was one policeman hereabout there
might be others. It seemed expedient to hasten
back to Dirksen and his followers and warn them
that there could be danger ahead.

'What're you going to do now?' he asked the two
youngsters.

Joe Tooley, mounting his horse said: 'We aim to
get the hell out of here fast.' He had no intention
of giving anything like a straight answer to this
unsavoury-looking pair. If they learned that there
were three corpses not far away – corpses probably
with money, watches and other valuables on their
persons – as well as three horses carrying saddles,
trappings and weapons, they might well kill the
brothers to avail themselves of the rich pickings.

His brother followed his lead and took to his
saddle. 'Yeah, pretty damn fast,' he affirmed. The
pair turned their animals' heads to ride back along
the trail.

Fluter and Diggs were relieved. This pair, for all
they were all tricked out as desperadoes, were
young and plainly raw and badly scared.

Though they posed no danger to a couple of old
dyed-in-the-wool outlaws such as themselves,
neither Fluter nor Diggs wanted these edgy kids to
hang around and attempt to join up with Kid
Dirksen' s crew and eventually prove a couple of
liabilities.

'Well, good luck to you,' said Diggs with little

sincerity as the two spurred their horses and headed back into the gloom.

Fluter and Diggs spent some time searching the darkening trail for a few more yards and discovered a spot close to a stream feeding the river. It offered graze for the horses of Dirksen's raiding party and had the making of a reasonable site for an overnight camp for the already weary and hungry gang.

'This place will do,' confirmed Fluter. 'Let's get back to the others pronto.'

They hastened back and reached Kid Dirksen and the remainder of the party as full night fell. Fluter quickly told Dirksen what they had learned from the Tooley brothers.

Dirksen looked alarmed. 'A policeman and a guy with panniers on his horse, you say?' he snorted.

He too had memories of a man whose horse carried panthers – the one who had surprised him at the waterhole when he had not yet fully recovered from the wound inflicted by the homesteader woman just before he deserted Dal Colquitt's gang.

Abruptly, the whole scenario of the drama at the homestead came back. In vivid detail, his brain replayed the young woman's defiant stand.

CHAPTER EIGHT

ECHO OF A SLAYING

When the Colquitt gang, to which Kid Dirksen was a recent recruit, jogged into the yard of the Blue Brush homestead, Dirksen's secret plans were already laid and in motion. He set out to take over the gang's secret headquarters at The Hole in the Choctaw Nation and his group of selected desperadoes would even at that moment be on their way to rendezvous in Salt Pass.

Kid Dirksen figured he had brains above the average and his brainwork had put together a plot which was to be implemented by his selected bunch of hard cases. It offered nothing more than a takeover of Dal Colquitt's lawless operations and his hidden headquarters. There was the additional blandishment of the loot from the Colquitt outfit's earlier robberies being concealed in The Hole, there for the taking and sharing out. That was a reckless promise on Dirksen's part for he did not know whether such loot even existed, but he could not resist dangling the prospect of a divvying-up of ill-gotten gains as a further enticement to the recruits.

Right after this diversion in the Colquitt gang's raiding spree, the purpose of which was to grab grub and water, Dal Colquitt planned to swing over to Rock City and hit its bank. Kid Dirksen would not be with them. He planned to desert on the trail and head back across the Red River and the Salt Pass rendezvous.

Dirksen thought sardonically that the Colquitts were welcome to what awaited them in Rock City – a welcome from well-prepared lawmen and citizens, alerted by Dirksen's anonymous letter to the Texas Rangers.

Then the raid on the homestead went all awry after the initial firing of some shots at the front of the house by way of a scaring calling card; this was all Dal Colquitt allowed in raids on homesteads, which were always for grub, arms or ammunition, for there was a peculiarity about Colquitt's approach to villainy.

Vicious-minded though he was, Colquitt always emphasized that there was hardly any need for too much rough stuff at such insignificant little places. Curiously, Colquitt, as unsaintly a desperado as ever caused mayhem in the blood-spattered history of

Texas, could show uncommon concern for the common people.

Colquitt's enemies were the law, the banks, the big ranchers and the grasping land companies who were beginning to have too much sway. Some said Colquitt turned bad because he had a hard-scrabble childhood of near starvation, backed by bitter experiences as a soldier of the defeated Southern Confederacy and he detested those who had plenty and waxed even fatter.

It turned out that there was no man on the homestead. Instead, a woman emerged. Undeterred by the shots that splintered the woodwork at the front of the house, she boldly levelled a Winchester rifle as she came down the steps of the porch.

She was youngish, slim with long blonde hair, a desirable woman – except for the menacing weapon she handled with obvious competence.

'Get the hell off this place!' she called. 'Go on – get!'

The Colquitts had drawn rein only yards in front of her. Kid Dirksen was riding his calico mare next to Dal Colquitt at the fore of the party. The woman swung the mouth of the Winchester directly towards him, perhaps because of his deceptively youthful appearance. Possibly she did not want to menace Dal Colquitt, a long-in-the-tooth villain who, equally deceptively, looked like a relatively harmless old man.

'Get off the place!' repeated the homesteader

woman, and she hoisted the weapon a little higher to point it unwaveringly at Dirksen's head. She looked as if she was about to trigger it.

Dirksen reacted to the menace. He clawed for his six-gun, hauled it from leather and fired at the woman. He heard her gasp. Then she fired the Winchester and a vivid blossom of fire flared in Dirksen's face.

He swerved instinctively to one side in his saddle and felt the bullet slice at his right temple, sending his senses spinning.

Half-stunned, he slid further over, fought to remain in the saddle, aware that blood was running down the right side of his face and dimly conscious of Dal Colquitt's rasping voice bawling: 'You damn fool! You've killed her! There was no need for that!'

The homesteader woman lay motionless, a pool of blood spreading from under her. Dirksen remained in his saddle, holding his head as his senses whirled.

The rest of the gang went into the house, took what food they could find, watered their horses at the trough beside the building, then filled their canteens. Without stopping to examine her, they left the young woman sprawling at the bottom of the porch, still clutching the Winchester, a corpse as far as they were concerned. They rode off at speed. The raid on Rock City was their next concern.

Dirksen kept up in the rear of the bunch with blood dripping from his wound. He managed to fashion a crude bandage from a portion of cloth

114

ripped from his shirt as the riders beat their retreat.

When his head cleared and he was thinking lucidly, Dirksen knew that, quite apart from furthering his own devious plan, he must now desert the Colquitts as quickly as possible. His wound appeared to be simply a graze, although bleeding profusely. It was rumoured that Dal Colquitt had, in the past, dealt brutally with a man seriously wounded in a gun battle. Rather than have him hinder the gang in making a swift getaway, Colquitt had shot him in his sleep. Dirksen had no intention of falling victim to such a fate.

As it was, he was only too aware of Colquitt's frequent hostile glances in his direction. The shooting of the homesteader woman sat uneasily on the gang leader who had such conflicting values.

As the gang was busy making night camp en route to Rock City, bedding down after watering their horses at a convenient stream, Dirksen lingered at the water longer than the rest, with his animal still saddled and laden with trail gear. It was almost too easy to sneak away, leading his calico mare into a thickly grown grove of trees.

He lit out northward towards the river, with the rendezvous at Salt Pass in Indian Territory as his goal.

Later in his journey, he glimpsed the man with the panniers after he stopped to rest at an obscure waterhole.

It was reasonable to suppose that the Texas Rangers had by then acted on the treacherous letter he wrote about the gang's intended raid at Rock City. He fired a hasty, panicky shot at the pannier man, believing he might be a Ranger who, in the aftermath of a debacle at Rock City, had caught up with him as a fleeing member of the Colquitts, not knowing that he was the author of the letter that betrayed the gang.

He had never mentioned this mysterious man to any of the newly formed gang.

Lafe Fluter, likewise, kept quiet about his run-in with the pannier man. To cover his arrival at Salt Pass without his sidekick, Charlie Clashman, he had concocted an elaborate lie.

Fluter claimed that he and Clashman were jumped on the trail by half a dozen desperadoes intent on robbery and that the mythical assailants killed Clashman while Fluter escaped by the skin of his teeth after heroically but vainly defending Clashman.

It would never do to allow Dirksen to know that he and Clashman, supposedly among the élite of bank robbers, were so stupid and blundering as fatally to bungle an easy job like overpowering a lone traveller who appeared to be at their mercy.

For both Dirksen and Fluter, the man with the panniers was an enigma, and Dirksen was particularly concerned by the rumour that he was in the company of a policeman of some kind. Was he perhaps one of the United States Indian Police whose proper jurisdiction lay across the Red River in Indian Territory? Had the Indian force and the

Texas Rangers caught on to his recent activities on both sides of the river?

Had both bodies put a joint force on his trail? Perhaps the pair who killed the members of the party with which the two young fellows travelled mistook that party for Dirksen's newly formed outfit.

Dirksen's anxieties multiplied. If the law was out in force, caution was called for in this initial expedition of lawlessness.

In an unsettled mood, Dirksen led his men on to make night camp at the site selected by Fluter and Diggs. As Jim Wing had predicted, they were travelling white man's fashion: camping with a cooking-fire, food, smokes and such comfort as bedrolls on hard ground could provide.

By contrast, Wing and Lockhart were then making speedy progress through the Red River bottoms in stoic Indian fashion. With Wing setting the pace, they drove their horses as hard as was practicable.

Now and again, there were brief periods when the animals were watered at the river and allowed some respite so that their wind was not impaired, and Wing kept Lockhart alert, tutoring him in regulating their mounts in alternate bursts of galloping and fast trotting which was kept up through the night. Jim Wing was following the hard-riding traditions of the Indian Nations' original Light Horse bands of lawmen, out of which grew the more formal United States Indian Police.

At times, Lockhart found himself almost at one with the Indian psyche, not feeling the passing of time, close to a hypnotic dream and oblivious to the surroundings, the river scents and the night and yet somehow wholly in tune with the whole of creation.

Dawn broke in the wide sky and a bright new day opened with the pair riding up from the lower reaches of the river towards a just visible drift of blue smoke marking the position of the town of Squaw Crossing.

They hit the higher, better travelled trail into the town and urged more effort out of their near-jaded mounts.

Passing the expansive tract of land near the ford over the river where there was a series of fenced-off pens for holding cattle before they were driven out of Texas, Lockhart and Wing brought their lathered animals into Squaw Crossing.

The town was tranquilly and blissfully unaware that it was about to be targeted by an outlaw gang already awakened from its night camp, already in the saddle, fully armed, menacing and almost within striking distance.

CHAPTER NINE

BEEF ON THE HOOF

Lockhart and Wing came into town finding the stores not yet open and the main street deserted except, curiously in view of the hour, for Marshal Bill Ritter, who was standing outside his office with two younger men, each bearing the star of a deputy. Some distance behind them, close to the road leading out of town and southward, an impressively dressed, bearded man was sitting on a big bay horse. With him was a lean rider whose range gear was topped off by a wide sombrero.

Lockhart and Wing rode up to the lawman and his deputies and swung down from their lathered and steaming horses.

'Dave Lockhart!' called Bill Ritter. 'I'm sure surprised to see you. These two are Dick Maybank and Walt Blake, my deputies. You've arrived right when we have trouble on our hands and all unexpected.'

'This is Captain Jim Wing, of the US Indian Police,' stated Lockhart. 'You've got trouble for sure. We rode all night to tell you a gang of bank robbers is on the way here, aiming to strike just as soon as the bank is open.'

'What?' bawled Ritter. 'A raid on our bank – right when we have a herd about to come through town? Hell, we'll have our hands full enough in a matter of minutes without bank robbers showing up!'

'Can't help it, Marshal,' protested Lockhart. 'It's all too complicated to explain right now, but we know they're on their way and not far behind us. It's an outfit who've taken over the Colquitts' operation. Captain Wing and I split the wind all night to warn you to keep the women and kids off the street and to get the men ready to hold 'em off. Squaw Crossing men will have to do what the Rock City folk did to the Colquitts.'

Marshal Bill Ritter glowered at Lockhart and Wing as if he believed they had personally engineered the situation to bring him yet more pain and discomfort.

'Blast it, Lockhart, we were not due to have another herd through for days, then Colonel Holz, from the San Benito River country, showed up with a big herd he's put on the trail earlier than usual without any warning. That's him yonder with his foreman. They've just arrived in town ahead of the beef to warn us that the herd is only a couple of miles away and coming fast. If we get bank robbers on top of a herd moving through town there'll be hell to pay!'

The bearded rider and the big-hatted cowman, seeing the agitated exchange between Ritter and the men with him, trotted their animals over to them.

Colonel Holz was a large man who looked every inch the prosperous rancher.

'What's the trouble, Marshal?' he demanded.

'Just got word of a gang on the way here aiming to rob the bank, Colonel,' said Ritter. 'You'll have to hold your herd out of town for a spell until we deal with this crisis.'

'No!' spluttered the rancher. 'Delay my drive because of some damn fool rumour? Certainly not! There have been rumours of robbery all over Texas since the days of the Colquitts. Well, that gang is finished now and we can discount any rumours.'

'It's no rumour,' said Jim Wing firmly.

'These two men wouldn't spread alarm on a mere rumour,' affirmed Ritter.

'And I'm damned if I'll delay my drive,' growled Holz. 'I have to get this beef across the river and through the Indian Nations to the railhead pronto. It's a valuable army contract and I aim to deliver every horn, hoof and tail on time.'

'There are holding corrals on the way into town,' Ritter pointed out. 'You could drive your cattle into them until we get this robbery threat over with.'

'Nothing doing,' declared Holz adamantly. 'I don't believe there are any robbers on the way here and I never pen my beef in a trail town. That'll give my hands time to go drinking and gambling and you know I don't permit such behaviour. I employ trail crews to drive cattle, not waste time!' He wheeled his horse and he and his foreman trotted back to the other end of the street.

'Darned if that man isn't the most ornery, cantankerous old buzzard in all Texas,' muttered the exasperated Ritter.

He addressed his deputies urgently: 'Dick, Walt, just as soon as the stores open and there are people on the street, round up the men with as many guns as they can bring. Place them where they can do most harm to this gang and make sure there are no women and kids on the street.'

Only a few moments before, unnoticed by her father and his companions, Helen Ritter had crossed the main street, walking with dignity and fluid grace, employing her crutch with an easy skill acquired from long use. It was unusually early, the sun was yet low in the sky and Helen smiled, feeling quietly amused at the almost comic disgruntled mood of her father as, earlier, he left the little house they shared.

They had been awakened almost at dawn by Deputy Marshal Dick Maybank banging on the front door with a message that the always unpredictable Colonel Holz had suddenly appeared in town announcing that he was bringing a big herd in at almost any moment.

Bill Ritter contended that he could get along with every cowman in Texas but the imperious Colonel

Holz, who seemed to think the world should work by his rules. Once again, the cantankerous old rancher had disregarded the cattlemen's usual courtesy of giving Squaw Crossing decent prior notice before invading with hundreds of head of longhorns on their way to the Red River crossing. Bill Ritter bolted an inadequate breakfast and departed, spluttering and fuming, to join his two deputies and set about preparing the town for the arrival of the herd.

Helen, having risen early, remembered that, at her shop, she had an urgently ordered lady's costume partially cut and she decided to make an early start on the work before, as was usual with a drive, the town was clogged by moving cattle. She had just mounted the plankwalk outside her premises when she saw her father standing near his office with mounted Colonel Holz and his foreman and two more men. One was a tall, dark-clad Indian and the other, equally tall, was Dave Lockhart.

At the sight of him, Helen felt her heart lift. None of the men seemed to notice her since they were in earnest conversation and, for an instant, she had a strong impulse to cross the street and greet Lockhart but, wishing to avoid being entangled in an imminent torrent of moving cattle, she continued towards her shop. She resolved to catch up with Lockhart when the drive had gone through.

She tried to assure herself that she was merely interested in knowing what had happened to him since he departed from the town earlier, but that lift of the heart told her she was fooling herself. She wanted to be in the company of Dave Lockhart for himself alone.

In her shop, she set about completing the work already laid out on her cutting table behind the counter.

Only a short time after Squaw Crossing's dressmaker began plying her civilized trade of creating attractive attire, a group intent on far less civilized pursuits were on the edge of town.

Kid Dirksen and his band had halted and dismounted. The band had gathered around Dirksen, who was holding a sheet of paper. Dirksen had decided from the start that his gang would not employ the old and dangerous methods of the Colquitts, who simply rode into a town in force and terrorized the citizenry. He planned more subtle measures.

This was the initial raid of the new gang and Dirksen was out to make its debut on the stage of lawlessness a memorable one, with the employment of intelligent strategy.

Of particular concern to him was the tale picked up along the trail that the mysterious man with the panniers and a police officer were somewhere in this vicinity. He was still haunted by the thought that, possibly, the two were part of a stronger force of law active hereabouts and Dirksen was determined not to ride into some kind of trap. Vigilance and proper preparation were called for.

The paper in his hand was a crude map drawn by

Lafe Fluter, the only member of the gang who had taken a close-up view of the bank in Squaw Crossing. Fluter had cast his professional eye over it while passing through with his erstwhile partner. Though light on brains, Fluter had a natural talent for assessing the vulnerability of banks. Like a general plotting his actions on a battlefield, he took note of a bank, its location and the points from which it might best be approached and entered as well as the lie of the land for making a speedy getaway.

His scrawling showed the bank on the corner of a minor street branching off the town's main street while a narrow alley ran on its other side.

The only entrance faced the main street. Together, Dirksen and Fluter had worked out the strategy of the raid with Dirksen emphasizing his dictum that every man had a job and each one stuck to it.

Now, at this trailside conference in the broadening light of the new day, he outlined the moves.

'Remember, the town will hardly be awake,' he said. 'There'll be no riding into the place in a group. That'd be as good as sounding an alarm,' he stipulated.

Fluter's sketch map was detailed enough to show that the narrow alleyways between the clapboard buildings of the main street led out to the open land outside the town. Consequently, riders need not use the main entrance to the town that also led to the river crossing. They could make more concealed inroads to the main street by cautiously riding through the alleys.

'We'll go in a couple at a time, by way of different alleys, so we don't arouse suspicion,' said Dirksen. 'Ride around, keeping close to the bank and two of you get into that little street and two in the alley. Just as soon as someone opens up the bank, the four from the street and the alley will crowd in with guns ready, taking him by surprise, shoving him right into the bank.'

He gave a detailed plot of who would make the first moves, who would go for the safe, who would rifle the tills and who would guard the outside and keep the horses of participants under control.

The planned getaway would be swift and by way of the southern road into town, with a wide swing back north and over the Red River.

'Only shoot if you have to and if we do this without noise, we'll clean out the bank and be gone before this gopher hole of a town has properly opened its eyes,' Dirksen boasted. Not that he had any aversion to killing, but he wanted the Dirksen gang's very first calling-card to be delivered in an action far slicker and brainier than the crude rampagings of the Colquitt outfit, whose strategy had been rooted in that of the rebel guerrilla bands of the Civil War.

So the men checked their weapons and thumbed cartridges into the chambers of their six-guns and replenished the magazines of their carbines.

Back in town, Helen Ritter was busily sewing when she heard running feet. The window near her work table gave her a view of the street and she saw Deputy Walt Blake run past her shop. After a brief spell, he reappeared, running back with a drawn revolver, followed by three townsmen, each carrying a weapon.

Undoubtedly, something was brewing and she watched the street intently, eventually seeing a couple of citizens, bearing rifles, appear on the roof of the store opposite her premises. Helen continued working while eyeing the window with her thoughts on her father. Something was clearly about to happen when the local men were turning out with firearms, and any sort of gun trouble in the town was bound to involve its chief lawman. Her father was such a determined old warhorse, he was likely to plunge into action. In a fight, worries for his own skin would be the last concern of Marshal Bill Ritter.

At that very moment, Marshal Ritter, his pair of deputies and Lockhart and Jim Wing were running around various parts of town, rousing anyone willing to mount an armed stand against the expected raiders and placing them in strategic positions.

Within ten minutes the lawmen had gathered a substantial force. Civic pride was running high in Squaw Crossing. The townsmen were determined to defend their property and more than one Civil War veteran was beginning to feel again the edgy challenge of battle.

Armed storekeepers and tradesmen established themselves behind barriers of barrels and packing cases dragged on to the plankwalks on either side of the street; others were sprawled on rooftops as snipers and the blacksmith, Tom Simmons, was positioned at the door of his forge, levelling a Sharps rifle at the main outlet to the river road, by which the raiding band was expected to enter.

Beside him, strategically placed to have a good view of the arrival of the gang by that route, was grizzled old Bob McCourt, owner, publisher, editor and sole reporter of the *Squaw Crossing Banner*. He had a Colt .45 at one side and a notebook and pencil at the other and was intent on providing his paper with the best front-page story of its life.

Lockhart and Wing had stabled their horses behind Ritter's office, leaving them saddled and rigged for immediate use in any subsequent chase.

Then, with Ritter and his two deputies, they plunged into organizing the defences.

Lockhart and Ritter concentrated on safeguarding the river road entrance while Wing and the deputies took up stations near the bank further along the street. The river-road end of the street was also covered by rooftop snipers. Squaw Crossing reckoned it was tight as a drum.

As the sun rose, tension mounted. Then a couple of riders suddenly trotted briskly out of one of the alleys. The sunlight touched naked weapons in their hands as they urged their horses easily towards the bank on a seemingly deserted street.

The defenders now saw that their elaborate defences were proving not so drum-tight. The alleys between the main street and open land fringing the town were unnoticed, vulnerable spots and the enemy was arriving in town stealthily.

Somebody on a rooftop fired and missed, sending a spurt of dust rising beside a hoof of a marauder's horse. The Dirksen riders, alarmed, spurred their mounts and lunged towards the cover of the alley flanking the bank.

Marshal Bill Ritter, at the further end of the street, snarled: 'Hell, they're coming in through the alleys. I never thought to keep them covered. That damned ornery Holz threw my thinking all to blazes.'

He saw the two raiders disappearing speedily into the alley. The town's defences were proving less tight than the defenders had thought.

And, at the very moment, the first shot was fired, Colonel Holz's herd moved.

The rancher's unreasoning behaviour fuelled the lawman's frustration. For, from the southern entrance to the street, came a pounding of hoofs that mounted to a thunder-roll.

Holz's herd had arrived just in time to be spooked by the single, echoing shot and a torrent of charging, bawling and grunting Texas longhorns was let loose, stirring up a fog of dust.

The herd spilled into the street, clogging it, cutting it off into two separate sections, impeding any chance of anyone knowing where the Dirksen gang were but, at the same time, splitting up the gang and scuppering their designs on the bank. With the point riders, galloping, wheeling their horses on the fringes of the drive, the animals raced for the road leading to the river crossing.

Marshal Ritter spluttered and swore into his big moustache. He blundered along the plankwalk, spitting mouthfuls of dust and growling: 'This beef is running like all hell! The damned fool who fired that shot did it right at the moment Holz brought his herd in. They're hog-wild – Holz's men can hardly hold them!'

Holz's action in pushing his trail herd into the town had totally frustrated the plan of Ritter and his allies in tackling the invasion of the Dirksen gang just at the moment when it was realized that they had reached the main street by way of the alleys between the buildings.

Now, against a backcloth of moving cattle and a mist of gritty dust, Holz's riders were trying vigorously and desperately to prevent a full-blown stampede.

The scene on the street became chaotic. There was no telling where the members of the scattered gang were and, even if any were spotted, it would be highly dangerous to open fire for fear of accidentally hitting any of the rancher's wranglers or further spooking the animals.

Bill Ritter had lost contact with his principal allies in organizing resistance against the raiders. He staggered across the plankwalk, spitting dust and cursing indignantly. He pressed himself against the clapboard wall of a store and stumbled through the dusty fog with his six-gun in his hand, then halted as he saw a tall, dust-obscured figure, likewise bearing a revolver, just ahead of him. The lawman cocked his weapon and went cautiously forward until the figure resolved itself into Dave Lockhart who, like Ritter, was taking refuge from the fury of the running cattle.

Up until the abrupt arrival of Holz's herd, Lockhart had been scouting the street with one object in mind – to find Dirksen. He saw nothing of him, and now his quest looked utterly hopeless.

'Dave!' called Marshal Ritter. 'I almost fired on you. I thought you were one of Dirksen's men. That damned Holz has loused up everything for us.'

'Can't do a thing until this run is over,' shouted Lockhart. 'Dirksen's gang can sneak into town under cover of this blamed swirling dust. The only consolation is that the bank will still be locked. The staff won't have opened up because of all this disruption. . . .' He broke off and stared into the fog of dust.

Half-obscured, a big man was blundering along, trying to get away from the thundering herd. Stumbling almost drunkenly, he reached the plankwalk.

Lockhart rubbed dust from his eyes and glowered through the gritty haze to verify the man's identity, then he gave a growl of satisfaction and said:

'Pardon me, Marshal, but here comes a gent I'm just hankering to welcome!'

He leapt into action and, waving his Colt high, he plunged off the wooden sidewalk to grab the front of the big man's buckskin vest with his free hand. Grinning like a demon and taking the unsuspecting man totally by surprise, he hauled him forward on to the planks of the walkway.

CHAPTER TEN

BOTTLED-UP OUTLAWS

Big Lafe Fluter was unhorsed when Holz's herd came charging into Squaw Crossing's main street. Having entered town by an obscure alleyway, the Dirksen gang's bank robbery specialist was riding audaciously across the hoof-pocked and wheel-rutted surface with the bank in his sights when a shot split the morning air and, as if it was a signal, a fury of tossing longhorns came charging directly at him.

Fluter's startled horse halted, then jumped, throwing an equally startled Fluter from his saddle. As the animal bolted, Fluter hit the ground, rolled, realized that he was full in the path of the pounding herd. With a desperate effort, he managed to haul himself up and stagger forward to grab an upright post supporting the awning over a plankwalk. In his panic, he had put himself on the further side of the street from where his fellow Dirksen riders had infiltrated the town, and Lockhart and Ritter were sharing this region with him. The gathering surge of cattle made a barrier, dividing them from the other part of the town and hemming them into a relatively small area.

With speeding cattle and a sea of dangerous horns passing within yards of him, Fluter fought for his breath in the smothering blanket of risen dust. He spat dust, turned around and was attempting to stride on to the plankwalk when an indistinct form lunged out of the veil of dust, gripped his vest and yanked him up on to the planks.

Fluter had a confused glimpse of his nemesis, the man with the panniers whom he and Charlie Clashman had tried to overpower at his night camp and who had twice cracked him over the head with a six-gun. Then, for a third time, a weapon descended forcefully on the crown of his hat and he was rendered cold yet again.

Lockhart dragged the unconscious man along the boards to Marshal Bill Ritter and dropped him in a heap at the lawman's feet.

'He's one of the Dirksen gang,' he yelled over the drumming and bawling of the running cattle. 'Get him into your cell when it's possible, Marshal. I want to see him in a court. He and his partner tried to kill me and I killed his partner. When the law gets the full story of what they aimed to do out of him, it'll show I acted in self-defence.'

Ritter's dust-coated face split into a grin. 'Well, at last, something's going our way,' he declared. From his back pocket he produced a pair of handcuffs and, with the toe of his boot, he rolled the still form of Fluter over on to his stomach, hauled his arms behind him and secured the handcuffs. He dragged Fluter across the walk and deposited him behind a packing-case outside a store.

'He'll keep there until we get this business over with,' he grinned with satisfaction.

Meantime, the mounting turmoil on the street totally distracted Helen's work. The single shot that sparked off the surge of cattle, the dinning of hundreds of rushing animals, the yelling of Holz's cowpunchers, caused her to leave her worktable and cross to the window for a closer look at the scene outside.

She knew about the arrival of Colonel Holz with his herd but had no knowledge of the Dirksen gang's designs on the bank, though the sight of the deputy and townsmen running and bearing firearms and of other armed men positioning themselves on rooftops warned her that something ominous and potentially deadly was happening in tandem with the arrival of Holz's trail-herd.

From the window she saw a blanket of hoof-risen dust through which the swiftly moving river of cattle appeared ghostly. Occasionally, in the background, there were equally ghostly drovers on horseback, rearing and wheeling, attempting to quieten the speeding, jostling longhorns.

Her long experience of life in this trail town told her that this herd was badly scared and the street was dangerous. She worried about her father, out there in that hazardous fury. Earlier, she had been amused by his complaining and spluttering mood, something his old enemy Colonel Holzt provoked every time he showed up with a herd. But, now, an uglier mood cloaked the town.

Something dangerous involving gunplay was unfolding out on the street behind the drama of the rush of cattle and her father, being a dogged old warhorse and a stickler for duty, would be involved in it up to his neck. He was no longer young but that was something to which he never paid any heed.

Helen's dread was that he would meet disaster out there in the hazardous chaos on the street.

She was concerned about Dave Lockhart, too, and the Indian in whose company he seemed to have arrived. She wondered what had befallen him since he stood right there in her shop, standing by the door, bidding her farewell, making a gallant and determined and yet lonely figure. Why was he back here in Squaw Crossing? Yet again, she had the urge to see him and be with him again. That unaccustomed lift of the heart returned and, guiltily, she realized that her thoughts were tending more to Lockhart than to her father.

At that moment, Dave Lockhart, with his hat pulled low to shield his face from the risen dust, was standing on a plankwalk that was reverberating with the pounding of the running herd.

The volume of the rushing animals seemed to be diminishing. Soon, there might be a sufficient dwindling of their numbers to allow him to dash across the street in the direction of the bank from which he had hitherto been cut off by the herd.

He wanted to locate one man among the Dirksen gang – Dirksen himself.

So far as he could tell, Fluter was the only gang member to be found on his present location in the street. The others who had used the alleyways to enter the town must be somewhere beyond the herd in the region of the bank – unless the unexpected charge of Holz's cattle had caused them to abandon their robbery plans and bolt out of Squaw Crossing the way they entered. They could do it easily under the distraction caused by Holz's herd.

Lockhart's ire rose at the unthinkable prospect of losing Dirksen after a pursuit up and down the Red River that concluded with an almost certain chance of settling his grievance against the baby-faced killer here in Squaw Crossing. He intended to take that chance fully and mercilessly if Dirksen could be found.

'If Dirksen has vamoosed, it'll be due to that blasted Holz,' he fumed to himself. 'Why didn't he corral his beef outside town like Marshal Ritter asked?'

He was joined by Ritter, in equally fractious

mood. 'This run is slowing, Dave,' he shouted. 'Looks like this is the tail-end of 'em.'

Sure enough, a loosely strung-out squad of cowpunchers passed, accompanying a more controlled section of cattle and Ritter called: 'Hey, are you fellows the drag crew?'

'Sure thing,' responded a rider. 'These are the last of the herd. There's only the chuck wagon and supply wagons to come.' He spurred his horse on and the dwindled string of cattle tramped onward towards the outlet to the river in calmer fashion.

The canvas-covered chuck wagon rumbled by with a couple of supply wagons following.

'You can tell Colonel Holz to go to hell, Cookie!' shouted Marshal Ritter to the bearded old-timer driving the chuck wagon. 'And tell him I aim to find a way of banning his blasted outfit from this town. He'll have to cross the Red elsewhere in future!'

'I'd tell him gladly, Marshal – except he'd fire me!' called the grinning cook as the creaking vehicle rocked away over the uneven surface of the street.

'C'mon, we can get further up the street now,' urged Ritter. 'Too bad we got cut off by that herd. If Dirksen's gang are still in town, they're somewhere up that way. The only one of the bunch I've seen down here is the one you beaned, now sleeping peacefully back yonder.'

'I reckon he was running for it under cover of that near stampede,' answered Lockhart. 'If the others are around they must up the street near the bank and Wing and your deputies must be up that way – that's where the shot came from. Something was going on up that way before that shot started the beef running.'

Right on cue, a shot, quickly followed by another broke the silence left after the thundering and bawling of the cattle. They came from the further end of the street which Lockhart and the lawman were hitherto unable to reach because of the barrier of moving animals.

At once, the two jerked into action and began to run towards the sound.

Marshal Ritter put on a spurt of speed, showing agility and energy in spite of his years. With their guns drawn, they kept close to the sides of the buildings lining the planked sidewalk, with their eyes on a drift of gunsmoke showing near the corner where the bank stood.

Across the street, they saw Captain Jim Wing lying belly-down on the plankwalk with a Winchester levelled towards the bank. Deputy Dick Maybank was a short distance away behind a set of barrels outside a store, levelling a Colt revolver. Further up the walk, Deputy Walt Blake, lying on the planks, also had the region of the bank covered with a carbine.

'They're in the alley and the street beside the bank – Dirksen included,' shouted Wing. 'They bolted in when that stampede started. Probably figured there were two ways out of town but they were wrong. There are fences built across the other end of the street and the alley. We've got 'em totally covered – us and the guys on the rooftops. They have no hope of getting into the bank; it just didn't open up with all that danger on the street. We told 'em to surrender but they're slinging lead at us.'

'I'm coming to join you!' shouted Lockhart, launching himself from the plankwalk at a run.

He zigzagged across the street, hearing Maybank's warning: 'Watch your step!' a second before a couple of shots spat from the direction of the bank and spouts of earth erupted behind him. Reaching the plankwalk, he flattened himself beside Wing.

'Give yourselves up, you damned fools!' bawled Jim Wing to Dirksen's men. 'You're outnumbered and in a hole. We'll get you in the end!'

Another defiant shot sounded from the alley beside the bank and hot lead slammed into one of the barrels sheltering Dick Maybank.

In the alley, Kid Dirksen was cursing his luck. Still saddled on his calico mare, he was rueing the wild action he and his followers had taken just as Holz's herd began to charge down the street right at the moment they were advancing on the bank.

All the gang, except the two who had initially crossed the street to enter the alley beside the bank made a horseback dash out of the alleys on the opposite side of the street and gained the one flanking the bank. They succeeded because the Squaw Crossing men guarding the street and positioned on the rooftops had been taken by surprise by the unexpected onrush of cattle following the ill-timed shot that spooked the animals. It was in this dash that Fluter was unsaddled and had to run wildly for his life.

Now, Dirksen and four of his men were holed up with their mounts in the alley alongside the bank. Two more had made it into the street on the other side of the building.

Other streets and alleys leading off the town's major street led to open land, but these two ended blindly, blocked by stout fencing, a point missed by bank robbery specialist Lafe Fluter when he and Charlie Clashman made their cursory assessment of the town.

The near stampede had totally disrupted the morning routine of the town.

No one came to open up the bank and be quickly overpowered before Squaw Crossing was fully awake. Instead of a few sleepy townsfolk beginning the day, there were charging cattle and warlike citizens on the street. Dirksen and his bunch were now in a tight corner.

The leader of what he had hoped would be the newest collection of unstoppable desperadoes on the Texas scene had seen his prior planning and smart strategy disintegrate. And he and his henchmen were trapped.

The baby-faced outlaw growled obscenities and checked the magazine of his Winchester, then pumped the weapon. He turned to his companions, some of whom were still sitting on their mounts

141

while others were afoot and huddled against the wall of the bank.

'C'mon,' he urged. 'Mount up and we'll make a dash clear across the street, shooting as we go. Make for that side street opposite. It leads to open land. We'll get the hell out of this blasted town!'

'Hell, Kid, we'll never make it!' objected one. 'There's too many of 'em out there. We're bottled up!'

Looking down from his saddle, Dirksen saw that those holed up with him were cowering within the cover of the narrow alley and showing no inclination to follow his desperate order.

He remembered the two gang members separated from his own group, now taking cover in the street on the further side of the bank.

Hoping his voice would carry to them, he yelled hoarsely: 'Hey, you guys in the street, we're making a run for the alleyway over the main street, smoking it out as we go. Follow me as soon as you see me!'

Answer came from the other side of the building: 'It's too chancy, Kid. It looks like certain death. None of us are risking it. The damned town's stiff with guns and we wouldn't have a hope.'

All of those grouped behind Dirksen, mounted or afoot, looked intent on not budging. His hand-picked crew of desperadoes were looking decidedly yellow.

'Damn it, you're turning out to be a bunch of gutless jail-sweepings!' he spat. 'Well, I'm not staying here to be smoked out by a set of storekeepers and clerks! And I'm damned if I'm surrendering. We can get out of here if we make the effort in a body. We can charge across the street and get clear, make it over the river and back to the Choctaw Nation and The Hole.'

'Getting back on tired horses is a tall order, kid,' hooted one man. 'Why should we go back?'

There was sharp cunning written all over Kid Dirksen's face as he replied: 'Why, have you forgotten what's waiting back there – all that loot left by the Colquitt crew? It's all waiting to be shared out.'

'We heard you talk of Colquitt loot in The Hole,' declared another man. 'Hell, you recruited the bulk of us on the strength of that kind of talk but we've heard damned little about any share-out since. More than one of us doubts you, Kid. Do you know where the loot is?'

'Boys, I do know and I always aimed to share out everything in our hands after a few successful capers of our own,' answered Dirksen on a note of injured innocence. 'What with what we grab on our own account and the Colquitt loot, the whole bunch of us can light out for Mexico and live like kings down there. Make a dash for it. We can be across the street and out of town quicker than these hicks can squeeze their triggers.'

Dirksen's whole strategy was to look after himself and to move with enough guns backing him up in an escape dash to give him every chance of preserving his valuable skin. The chances of the

143

outlaw bunch making it back to The Hole were slim indeed, but his appeal to greed began to affect the criminal minds surrounding him.

'Maybe we should try it,' wavered one voice.

'Yeah, maybe we should,' assented another.

The mood began to catch on under the spur of greed for the supposed Colquitt loot which had assumed almost mythic proportions in the avaricious minds of the gang. Soon the whole bunch were shaking off their lethargy and there was a general scuffling of boots and creaking of leather as the men bottled up in the alley began to remount.

'You men in the street – we're charging out and shooting as we go,' bawled Dirksen. 'You'd better join us. It's our only chance. Ride when I shout!'

Outside, tension was climbing while the townsmen, with ready trigger fmgers, awaited a move from the outlaws.

'Now!' came Dirksen's hoarse yell.

With the Winchester levelled, he kneed his mare into a desperate, dead-run out of the alley and on to the street, opening fire wildly as soon as he was clear of the narrow passageway. The men he had won over came behind him like a bedraggled and undisciplined cavalry troop, shooting at random as they progressed in a dusty storm of pounding horses.

At once, there was a fusillade of firing from the defenders of Squaw Crossing. One outlaw screeched and pitched out of his saddle and, from the corner of his eye, Dirksen, at the head of the charge, saw that the courage of his men was all too short-lived; they were wheeling their mounts around and making hasty tracks back to the cover they had just left.

Cursing, with his head held low, Dirksen raced on alone, then a shot from among the townsmen drilled the skull of his calico mare. The animal lurched and pitched over, dead before it hit the ground.

Snarling breathlessly, Dirksen hurled himself out of the saddle, involuntarily flinging his rifle out of his grasp as he did so.

He smote the dust and narrowly missed being pinned under his fallen animal.

He rolled, fumbled for his holster and yanked his Colt from it even as he scrambled to his feet.

Seeing he was unprotected in the middle of the street, he began to hare for the plankwalk on the opposite side of the street to that occupied by the armed citizenry.

From that same point, Dave Lockhart sprang up from his position beside Jim Wing and ran from the plankwalk flourishing his handgun.

A red rage all but consumed him. He had been prevented from shooting Dirksen in the cavern of The Hole but now he had him within reach and he was determined on revenge. This time, Dirksen's life would not be spared. This time, Lockhart vowed, he would die – and die knowing why Lockhart was pumping hot lead into him.

145

As he gained his balance, Dirksen saw Lockhart charging towards him. The Squaw Crossing men deployed along the street, held their guns silent, watching the drama being enacted in the middle of the street but Jim Wing still called into the tension-filled air: 'Don't any of you men shoot! You might hit Lockhart!'

Dirksen's mouth dropped open with the recognition that the man charging at him was he of the horse panniers – the man who seemed to have been doggedly on his trail. He suddenly turned and started to run, six-gun in hand, making blindly for any kind of cover. Lockhart went running after him, thinking only of at last grasping a chance to put into action the scenario he had long and bitterly contemplated.

He wanted only to confront Dirksen face to face, and tell him with bloodthirsty relish that he was about to die in retribution for killing Marcy – then slay him.

Dirksen turned, saw his pursuer closing on him with his face a mask of vengeful fury. Lockhart's total determination seemed to communicate itself to him and he halted, twisted around, raised his Colt and fired.

Lockhart ducked the moment he saw Dirksen turn. A sharp stinging at his left shoulder followed the blast of the revolver and Lockhart stumbled. He had a confused vision of the street scene whirling about him including a blurred image of the sign over Helen Ritter's shop, announcing her name in its Frenchified form: *Helene*.

In the shop, Helen was at the window, watching with horror the enactment out on the street as though on a stage virtually on her doorstep. She saw Lockhart lurch then regain his balance. A leer of triumph spread over the youthful face of the man who had just fired at him but Lockhart kept staggering forward in his direction. The baby-faced man stood still, no longer a fugitive, but waiting with a ready gun for Lockhart to draw nearer and looking confident of killing him. Lockhart continued to approach unsteadily. Blood was beginning to soak his shirt at the shoulder.

With her face close to the window, watching in awe, Helen heard the youthful-faced man demand: 'Who the hell are you, mister? You've been on my tail and I want to know why.'

'I'm Lockhart, homesteader from Blue Brush,' called Lockhart harshly. 'Remember Blue Brush? You were there with the Colquitts. You killed my wife – and I aim to kill you!'

There was a sneering answering laugh. 'Sure I killed her. She was about to kill me, but I had big plans and no damned homesteader woman was going to louse them up. Too bad that she got off a lucky shot and grazed me. I took good care I gave her more than a grazing!'

Lockhart, with his face distorted by pain and fury, raised his gun decisively then staggered and, with his legs suddenly giving way under him, he fell forward into the dust, feeling searing pain at his shoulder. Dirksen levelled his own weapon at the fallen figure. Lockhart looked like easy meat and Dirksen figured he could take his time about killing him.

Helen gritted her teeth against a rising scream and reached for her crutch.

Out on the street, Dirksen was almost squeezing the trigger when a strong female voice rang from the plankwalk: 'You filthy scum!'

Dirksen turned and opened his mouth at the sight of Helen crossing the plankwalk from the door of her shop and heading for him in her nimble and speedy way. She halted, face to face with him, with her brows pulled down angrily over furiously blazing eyes.

'You miserable specimen!' she spat. 'Garbage like you should be cleaned off the street!'

CHAPTER ELEVEN

SHOWDOWN

Dirksen's jaw dropped further, then his surprise became something like amusement and he began to work his face into a derisive grin. He was being challenged by a mere woman and a woman who was apparently not fully able at that; one who required the support of a crutch. To him, it was laughable.

Helen went straight towards him, coming off the plankwalk with an unerring long hop on her sound leg. She was only a couple of feet from him and he began to snigger into her face. In his mingled astonishment and amusement, he had swung the mouth of his pistol away from Lockhart and had allowed it to slant downward, a detail Helen had been watching with the tail of her eye all the time she was approaching him. She was also taking careful account of the proximity of her crutch to Dirksen.

'Clean me off the street?' Dirksen sneered. 'Who's going to do it? You – a crip—?' He never finished the sentence.

Helen made a blurringly fast movement, swinging the crutch upward in an arc, perfectly calculated to smite the wrist of Dirksen's gun hand and jerk it up. He yelped and the cry blended with a barking blast from his Colt as he automatically triggered it harmlessly into the air before dropping it.

'You were about to use a word I find ugly,' Helen called icily. Then, balancing on one foot, she followed her action through, swivelling her body and swinging the crutch around laterally to deliver a bone-cracking blow to Dirksen's head.

He gave a choking gurgle and pitched over backwards.

Sprawling in the dust, Lockhart had a befuddled, inverted view of the whole action and he was aware of Dirksen's Colt landing somewhere close to him. He had dropped his own gun and did not know where it was. Shaking his head, striving for a clear grasp of reality, he rolled over on to his stomach, clawed blindly around his body, found Dirksen's weapon and grabbed it. He forced himself up to his knees then unwound his body slowly until he was standing.

Dirksen was lying on his back at his feet, twitching, half-conscious but making feeble attempts to rise and floundering without success. He rolled over with his eyes wide and his chin trembling as if gibbering soundlessly at the sight of Lockhart towering over him and aiming the revolver at his head.

Lockhart was now gripped by a blazing and all-consuming anger. He had a vision of himself on his knees, holding his dying wife and felt again his choking, tearful and enraged grief. Now, at last, he had the man responsible for her murder sprawling before him, totally his for the slaying.

He cocked the Colt and levelled it at Dirksen's head.

'Dave – no!' Helen's voice was an almost agonized shriek. 'Dave – not wanton killing!'

Lockhart saw Helen coming towards him, taking a long hop aided by her crutch.

She stopped and stood still with her practised ability to remain steadily balanced on her sound foot.

She raised the crutch and held its tip firmly under his gunhand, threatening to knock it upwards as she had Dirksen's hand.

'Please, Dave! Marcy wouldn't want it!' she said. 'Leave him to the law! Can't you see he's beaten? You'd be as bad as him if you kill him now. I heard him admit killing Marcy and I'll say so in a law court. Look around you. Half of Squaw Crossing also witnessed it. They'll testify, too.'

Lockhart froze, stilled by the quivering intensity of her cry. It quenched the fires within him and he thought that, in some uncanny way, Helen seemed to know Marcy better than he did himself.

True, his wife had made a stand with the Winchester, but it was in a proper defence of her home. Abhorrence of killing and brutality was part of the very essence of the girl he had loved so deeply. She always desired justice and fairness.

When he looked around, he saw that groups of the townsmen who had defended the town were gathered about, spectators of the drama he and Dirksen had staged.

He turned and looked at Helen, holding her determined pose with the raised crutch and saw that her intriguing eyes were fixed on him. There was a sudden, involuntary catch in his throat.

In Helen's eyes there was that very same look that he had seen so often in Marcy's eyes, an indefinable, luminous light assuring him that, without doubt, she loved him.

She held him with a near pleading gaze and spoke softly but firmly.

'Dave, I once told you I know that Marcy would want her man to be always just the man she married, and I know she didn't marry a cold-blooded killer.'

He lowered the gun, holstered it and clutched at his wounded shoulder, now causing blood to soak his shirtsleeve.

'You took a big chance,' he said huskily. 'He might easily have fired at you.'

Now Helen grinned at him like a mischievous youngster, but her eyes held that magnetically attractive glow that he knew was there for him alone.

She brought down her crutch, rested on it and gave it an approving pat.

'You were worth taking a chance for. Anyway, Peggy just took him by surprise. I told you she's a useful accessory for a girl to have in a cowtown.' She laughed. Then her mood changed abruptly when she took in the blood reddening the sleeve of his shirt. 'You need Doc Thornton, Dave. That wound must be attended to.'

'I'm right here,' said Doc Thornton, Squaw Crossing's only medico, a stooped, bearded old man in dusty broadcloth who came pushing his way through the spectators bearing a battered black bag. The doctor busied himself at once, squinting critically at the wound in Lockhart's arm.

'I've been hanging around knowing that, sooner or later, in all this hoorawing, someone would start yelling for a doctor,' he commented drily. 'Sit down on the edge of the sidewalk, son, and let me dress that shoulder.'

He ripped off the greater part of Lockwood's shirtsleeve in a businesslike way.

'You're lucky it's only a flesh wound,' he said.' The bone's not been hurt. There's a lot of blood but I reckon it's mainly shock that ails you,' he pronounced. 'A cleaning up, a sousing with iodine and bandaging should put it right.' He set to work with an anything but gentle vigour. Doc's methods were strictly those of the frontier but he claimed with some justification to have saved more lives than he lost.

As Doc Thornton worked on him, Dave Lockhart realized that a good portion of Squaw Crossing's population had formed an audience, witnessing the confrontation between himself and Kid Dirksen. Like a crowd at a prizefight, they stood well back, leaving an arena in which what they recognized as a bitter Western style grudge fight could be staged. Now, they were crowding in, congratulating Helen and Lockhart with the lion's share going to the town marshal's daughter.

Dirksen, half-conscious, had been hauled to his feet by Deputy Dick Maybank. Marshal Ritter and Captain Jim Wing shoved their way through the townsfolk from the direction of the lawman's office and lock-up.

'Walt Blake is back yonder, guarding a cell full of what's left of the sorriest looking badmen in Texas – including the big guy I cuffed earlier,' reported Bill Ritter.

'They just gave themselves up to us and a squad of citizens,' stated Wing in his deadpan Indian way. 'They had no fight in 'em even before Dirksen made a break to save his own skin. Not one had the guts of a jackrabbit. Dirksen mistook the quality of his prison sidekicks. They were no second Colquitt bunch.'

Bill Ritter, who had been otherwise engaged when Helen dealt with Dirksen, turned to his daughter, now bending over Lockhart, helping the doctor dress his wound.

'What's this I hear about you brawling on the

street, daughter?' he demanded.

'I can't help it, Dad. It's all due to having an old-style frontier lawman as an old man,' Helen laughed.

'It sounds like plumb unseemly behaviour to me,' growled Ritter with mock solemnity, 'but I reckon it can be classed as good citizenship. Come to think of, old Colonel Holz did us all a good turn by shoving his cattle through town the way he did. With all that disruption, he sure stopped Dirksen's bunch from even getting started on their robbing spree. On the whole, Holz is a fine fellow. No wonder he distinguished himself as an officer.'

'Doggone it, Dad!' gasped Helen, sounding as exasperated as her father. 'Only this morning you were fit to explode, calling the colonel the most cantankerous and unpredictable man in all Texas.'

'Well, it's easy to misjudge a man,' said Ritter, philosophically filling his pipe.

Helen blew out her cheeks in mock exasperation, then stood up and adjusted her crutch under her arm. 'I'm going into my place to fix coffee the way Mr Lockhart likes it,' she declared. 'And I reckon all Squaw Crossing should think about getting a meal. There can't be a soul in town who had a proper breakfast this morning.'

The coffee was indeed made the way Lockhart liked it when, a short time later, he sat with Helen at the small table in her shop. His shoulder was tightly bandaged and stinging from iodine and he wore a clean shirt donated by Deputy Walt Blake.

155

Helen sat opposite him, glad to take some refuge from the folk of Squaw Crossing who were making a heroine of her.

Lockhart said: 'I heard someone say the town should put up a statue to you. You did take a powerful risk, doing what you did.'

Helen poured more coffee. 'What else could I do? I didn't want Dirksen to kill you nor you to kill Dirksen. If you had, Dave, it would have been the ultimate in what I wanted to guard you against – bloodthirsty bitterness. I know you would never have lived with yourself afterwards. It might have been raw revenge but it wouldn't have been justice and you'd know it only too well. You'd have reduced yourself. Then, you'd no longer be the man Marcy loved and married. It was important to me that you remained the man I took you for from the start; an honest and brave man but, like most men, sometimes headstrong and needing restraint.'

'You're an understanding woman, Helen,' said Lockhart. Then, embarrassed, he realized he had extended his hand across the table and had rested it lightly on her hand. He lifted it but Helen quickly recaptured it, smiled shyly and said: 'I try to be. I understand bitterness because I've been guarding against it all my life.'

She paused and squeezed his hand tenderly, saying: 'I wanted desperately to guard you against it, too. You're much too good to end up a hurt and bitter man.'

They quickly released hands, their conversation

interrupted by the door being opened and Jim Wing entering.

'I'm riding out,' he announced flatly. 'I'm just about to rub my horse down, feed him and head back over the river.'

Lockhart stood up. 'Miss Ritter, you haven't been formerly introduced, this is—'

'Captain Jim Black Eagle's Wing, United States Indian Police, Miss Ritter. Not that anyone ever bothers with my full name,' interjected Wing with a military salute.

'Won't you stay awhile, Captain?' said Helen. 'The whole town is indebted to you, along with Mr Lockhart, here.'

'No, ma'am. I'm needed back in the Indian Nations. No offence intended to you as a Texas lady but Indian police are just about tolerated on this side of the Red River. The long wars against the Comanches produced prejudices aplenty. I hardly need tell you how some feelings run against Indians.'

'I know it and regret it,' said Helen reflectively. 'But maybe Squaw Crossing folk have been given very good cause to think again.'

Wing gave her one of his rare smiles and turned to Lockhart. 'There'll be a day in court for Dirksen and those in Marshal Ritter's cell. I'll send the Texas Rangers a written account of our fight with the Bexleys to clear up any enquiries they might make.'

Another of his rare smiles crossed his face and he added: 'Not that they'll worry much about the

Bexleys. It was self-defence and you were assisting a police officer who was being attacked. That carries weight with the Rangers even when it's an Indian policeman who's involved.'

He saluted again and, without further ceremony, made for the door.

'That,' declared Lockhart as Wing departed, 'is the man who has taught me the meaning of the old Texas saying about the high quality of a man who who's fit to ride the river with.'

'And what of you, now that you've finished riding the river?' Helen asked.

'Oh, back to Blue Brush to see if my brother-in-law has disposed of the homestead, though I doubt if I'll settle there again. Maybe I'll choose a real friendly place, Squaw Crossing for instance. This place has its attractions. Maybe I'll even revive the ambitions I once had,' he said.

They looked at each other in a moment of silence, each aware that their earlier rapport had returned, but now it was in far stronger measure.

Helen remembered their grasping of hands and Lockhart lost himself in contemplation of that enchanting glow in her hazel eyes while she knew again the exquisite lifting of her heart that made her almost breathless.

It lifted even higher when he said, softly: 'As for the immediate future, a letter addressed to me at Blue Brush post office will find me.'

'You mean you want to keep in touch?' She sounded incredulous.

'Of course. Why not? Do you think the woman who thought I was worth risking a bullet for is not worth keeping in touch with or something?'

'Well, I thought maybe – me being the way I am – needing Peggy and all. . . .' She stumbled around the subject of her maimed foot.

'Why should I have anything against Peggy? Have you forgotten how she saved my life?' he asked, grinning.

Helen's eyes were as luminous as her sudden smile. 'You're another man to ride the river with, Dave Lockhart,' she said quietly.

Whereupon, he reached out, embraced her and kissed her, knowing with solid certainty that Marcy would understand and approve.